Praise for Jon

"[A] perfect example of the 'write, don't think' maxim as Fosse instructed his students in the late 80s in Bergen, when this book was in the making."
—Catherine Taylor, *The Guardian*

"[Fosse] shows a playwright's flare for the carefully-orchestrated dramatic; Boathouse may feel almost entirely understated, even in its shattering conclusion... but it haunts deeply and profoundly."
—M.A. Orthofer, *The Complete Review*

"Deeply psychological." —Norman Erikson Pasaribu, *Asymptote Journal*

"Jon Fosse is a major European writer." —Karl Ove Knausgaard

"Fosse . . . has been compared to Ibsen and to Beckett, and it is easy to see his work as Ibsen stripped down to its emotional essentials. But it is much more. For one thing, it has a fierce poetic simplicity." —*New York Times*

"[T]he oddity of reading Fosse [is that] what threatens to be heavy proves lightsome. You put on your boots to wade through the mud and find yourself floating along." —Blake Morrison, *London Review of Books*

"I think of the four elder statesmen of Norwegian letters as a bit like the Beatles . . . Fosse is George, the quiet one, mystical, spiritual, probably the best craftsman of them all." —Damion Searls, *The Paris Review*

"Fosse's pared down, circuitous, and rhythmic prose skillfully guides readers through past and present." —*Publishers Weekly*

"He is undoubtedly one of the world's most important and versatile literary voices." —*Irish Examiner*

"The Beckett of the 21st Century." —*Le Monde*

"There is something quietly dramatic about Fosse's meandering and rhythmic prose . . . which has a strangely mesmerising effect."
—*The Independent*

Other Books by Jon Fosse
in English Translation

Jon Fosse

Boathouse

Translated from the Norwegian by May-Brit Akerholt

DALKEY ARCHIVE PRESS
Dallas, TX / Rochester, NY

Published by agreement with Regal Hoffmann & Associates LLC
and Winje Agency A/S, Norway

Translation copyright ©2017 May-Brit Akerholt

Support for this publication has been provided in part by grants from the
National Endowment for the Arts, the Texas Commission on the Arts, the
City of Dallas Office of Arts and Culture, the Communities Foundation
of Texas, and the Addy Foundation.

Paperback: 9781628971828
Library of Congress Cataloging-in-Publication Data:
Names: Fosse, Jon, 1959, author. | Akerholt, May-Brit, translator.

Classification: LCC PT8951.16.073 N3813 20171 DDC
839.823/74-dc23 LC record available at https://lccn.loc.
gov/2017035402.

Interior design by Anuj Mathur
Printed in Canada

Jon Fosse

Boathouse

I

I don't go out anymore, a restlessness has come over me, and I don't go out. It was this summer that the restlessness came over me. I met Knut again, I hadn't seen him for at least ten years. Knut and I, we were always together. A restlessness has come over me. I don't know what it is, but the restlessness aches in my left arm, in my fingers. I don't go out anymore. I don't know why, but it is several months since I was last outside the door. It is this restlessness. That is why I have decided to write, I am going to write a novel. I have to do something. This restlessness is killing me. Perhaps writing will help. It was this summer the restlessness came over me. I met Knut again. He had got married, had two daughters. When we were kids Knut and I were always together. And Knut left. I called his name, but Knut just left. A restlessness has come over me. I looked at his back. I didn't know what to say, I just saw Knut standing there, down on the road, and then he walked away down the road. I haven't seen him since. My friend Knut, I hadn't seen him for at least ten years, and then I saw him again this summer. Knut's wife. A yellow rain jacket. The denim jacket. Her eyes. Knut is a music teacher, came home for the holidays. I'm more than thirty years old, and I haven't made anything of my life. I live here, with my mother. It was this summer the restlessness came over me. I've never written anything before, not of my own free will, I suppose most people have, written letters, or even poems, but I've never written anything. It occurred to me, suddenly, that I might be able to write. I had to do something, the restlessness was too overwhelming. It occurred to me pretty suddenly that perhaps I should start writing, that was after the restlessness had come over me, I had to do something, had to keep the restlessness at bay. I've actually never thought about the possibility of writing. Not before this restlessness. It came over me again and again, the restlessness, especially in the evenings, they used to be the best part of the day, but now the evenings are so restless, so entirely restless. I had to find something to do, and so I decided to write. Perhaps writing will help, will keep the restlessness at bay. I don't know. But this restlessness, which I can't shake off, perhaps it'll become more bearable if I write. Perhaps everything will become different. In any case the writing might keep the restlessness at bay for a few hours. I don't know. Because this restlessness is unbearable, and that is why I'm writing this novel. I sit here. I am alone. I am here. It is this restlessness. I sit in the attic, in my house, and I write. I'm not feeling too bad, it was quite clever of me to think of writing a novel, I think it was, even if I have only just started to write. The restlessness is unbearable, that is why I should write. I sit here in the attic, have two rooms to myself, and I can hear my mother walking around downstairs. Through the floor I can hear the sounds of the television. My life is quite good really. I have my guitar. I have a stereo system, records. I have books. Not all that many books, but I still read a lot, although I mostly get the books I read from the library. I read a lot. I can hear my mother walking around down there. I live with my mother, although I'm more than thirty years old. My mother is not all that old. We get along quite well, really, have lived together all our lives. This summer I met Knut again. When we were kids, Knut and I were always together. I haven't made much of my life. My mother. She is walking across the floor down there. My mother gets her pension every month, she buys food and she cooks, she pays the regular bills, electricity, telephone, she keeps the house neat and tidy, washes my clothes, grumbles most of the time. And I haven't made much of my life. Perhaps that worries my mother, perhaps it doesn't, it probably doesn't worry her, she's in the habit of saying that I have to get myself a job, I can't sit up in the attic strumming a guitar, she says, but she grins when she says it, and I don't know if I should believe what she says or not, besides, I do a few things now and then, or at least I used to, before the restlessness came over me and I decided not to go out anymore, while before, I used to go out and do the shopping for her, chop the firewood, all winter I would get the firewood, in the autumn I would help her pick berries, I fished all the fish we ate, and occasionally I would even earn a bit of money, I have done the odd job in my time, and, most of the money I earned came from playing at dances, which I used to do quite a lot. I play the guitar, and a teacher at the local high school plays the accordion. His name is Torkjell. That's why we are called Torkjell's Duo. It's this restlessness, it just won't go away. Now I don't go out anymore. That means that I'm unable to maintain the rather modest income I used to earn. It also looks bad for the duo I used to be part of. I have said no to taking part in several playing jobs lately, and I don't want to go to rehearsals either. Torkjell's Duo. That is just how it is. Mostly we were playing at weddings, apart from the odd dance. Torkjell's Duo. That is what it says on the posters, almost always written with a broad red marker. It's this restlessness, and I have stopped going out. It has been a long time since I last went out. This summer I met Knut again, and I had not seen him for at least ten years, he was married now with two kids. Knut and I were always together. We played together, started a band together. Knut has become a music teacher. It was when I met Knut again that the restlessness came over me. Knut and I decided to start a rock band together. My friend Knut. He came home for a visit this summer. He and his wife and their two little girls. He has two daughters. I had not seen him for at least ten years. I watched Knut dance with someone he went to school with, they were in the same class. Knut has become a music teacher. This summer he came home. I met Knut this summer. That was when the restlessness came over me. I was walking down the road, was going to the library, it was a lovely summer's afternoon. Then I see him coming around a bend in the road, then I see Knut coming. I see Knut. I see Knut coming into view, around the bend. I have not seen him for at least ten years, and now Knut comes walking toward me. First Knut is coming, and I have not seen him for such a long time, it feels like a long time, then a woman comes walking, with short thick black hair, brown eyes, she is wearing a denim jacket, and behind her two kids are skipping along the roadside. I see Knut coming and Knut thinks this is something he has been dreading, but he knew it had to happen, meeting old friends, had to happen, of course, and I still look more or less the same, Knut thinks, and then he wonders what he's going to say to me, it's all such a long time ago, we used to do so much together, but what's he going to say, we probably don't have anything in common anymore, but he has to say something, talk, this is exactly what he has been dreading, Knut thinks, but we have shared a lot, the two of us, all the dances we used to play at, the girls, and that one time, that girl, it didn't mean anything, I became so shy afterward, nothing serious, just a misunderstanding, it was at a dance, after we had been playing, and as usual a couple of girls kept hanging around, too silly, I changed totally afterward, became shy, didn't want to play any more, Knut thinks, and he thinks that he's married now, I've never really felt comfortable around women, Knut thinks, but he's married now, he thinks, and it's all such a long time ago, what's he going to say, has to say something, has been dreading this moment, knew it had to happen, still, has to spend his holidays somewhere, he has long holidays, is a teacher, can't just stay at home either. Knut thinks that he has to get out of this somehow. He sees me coming closer. I saw Knut appearing around the bend, he's coming closer, and I think it's such a long time since I've seen him, so many years, such a long time ago, and I lift up my hand, wave at Knut, and he lifts up his hand, waves back. We both look slightly past each other, we come closer, we come to a stop, and I look at Knut, he looks at me, then he turns around, looks at the woman who comes up behind him, waits for her, she comes up alongside us, the kids are running toward us, now they stand there beside me, look up at me, and I feel that this isn't going to be as difficult as I thought, this could work out all right, the kids will make it all alright, and I look at the girls, ask what kind of girls are they then, and I look at Knut.

What kind of girls are we, one of them says, and both girls start to giggle.

Well, as you see the family's grown, Knut says, looks at me with grinning eyes.

Yes, you've been clever, I say, and Knut turns his head and says he'd like to introduce his wife, I don't think you two have met, he says, and she slips in front of him, holds out her hand, tells me her name, but her voice is so low that I don't catch it. I tell her that Knut and I used to spend a lot of time together when we were kids, played in a band together, and she says that Knut has told her about me, isn't my name Baard, she says. Knut interrupts and says yes, we used to have a lot of fun together, didn't we.

Those were the days, I say.

Yes, Knut says.

And the boathouse's down there, I say.

Yes, we spent a lot of time there, says Knut.

Almost every day, I say.

So the boathouse is still there, says Knut.

I nod.

And it's as unpainted and run-down as ever, Knut says.

It'll stand there like that till it falls down, I say.

But Svein of Leite is dead, Knut says.

A few years ago now, I say.

He was a weird one, Svein was, Knut says.

Pity you didn't make a record, Knut's wife says.

Knut laughs, and I have to grin myself.

Well, we didn't even get close, I say.

You used to play at local dances? his wife asks.

Yes, I say.

Not a lot, still, the band did get a few jobs, says Knut.

Can we go now? says one of the girls.

Well, it was nice to see you again, Knut says.

Nice to meet you, his wife says.

Let's go, one of the girls says.

Yes, we're going, Knut says.

This minute, the girl says.

All right, says Knut, and then he says that they'll probably stay for the whole summer, I know, don't I, that he's become a teacher, he says, and he laughs briefly, and then he says he's sure we'll run into each other again, and I nod.

We could go fishing, I say.

You fish do you, he says.

The odd evening, out on the fjord.

Are you going out tonight? he asks.

I'd say so, I say.

Come on Dad, the girl says.

And then there's a dance at the weekend, I'm playing with Torkjell.

That high school teacher?

I nod.

You still play then, Knut says.

Not very much.

Let's go, the girl says.

Yes, we've got to go, his wife says, and she nods to me, I nod back, then Knut and I say see you later to each other, say that we must catch up, and then I walk down the road, I'm going to the library, and Knut and his family walk off in the other direction, and Knut thinks that of course, it's always like that, she had to look at me in that way, and it was strange to see me again, Knut thinks, and really, I was just the same, I hadn't changed very much at all, was almost the same, that girl, that time, the jobs we got playing with the band, it's a long time ago, couldn't have turned out all that differently, and now he's married, Knut thinks, and I just live in the same old rut, live at home, play a little, it's the way I've always been, Knut thinks, and he thinks that he's married, has two daughters, got married two years ago. Knut thinks that he knew he had to meet me again, had been dreading it, he thinks, but they had to go on holiday somewhere, a long summer holiday, not much money to spend, his wife at home with the kids, expensive to keep a family, inevitable that he'd meet old friends again, he'd been dreading it, his wife, why did she have to look at me like that, in that way, Knut thinks, and I turn around, watch Knut's back, I watch as he walks along the road, he's probably going to The Co-op, and I think that he's probably happy that he has met me, and that it wasn't so difficult to talk to me, happy about that, I think, and I walk toward the library, but I change my mind, don't want to borrow any books after all, it's not really the day for

it, I think, so I turn around, start to walk home again, and I
keep thinking that I've met Knut again, it must be at least
ten years since we saw each other, it was strange to see him
again, I think to myself, strange that we should meet just
across from the boathouse too, where we used to play a lot
when we were kids, were there nearly every day, for many
years, I think, and I walk back home, thinking that I might
be seeing Knut and his wife again, I don't want to, mustn't
meet them, not now, I think. I walk back home. I asked Knut
if he wanted to come out on the fjord with me, come fishing
with me, but he didn't answer, and that was actually what I
was hoping, that he shouldn't answer, that he shouldn't come
with me, I didn't really want us to go fishing together, just
felt I had to ask, felt it was the right thing to do, I couldn't
just say see you later, had to make some plans, plan something
I'm sure we both in fact didn't want to happen, it's so long
since we were together, many years, and we haven't seen each
other for such a long time, before I, that day, this summer,
saw Knut appearing around a bend, first Knut, then his wife,
then two girls. I hadn't seen him for many years, ten years at
least. And I was feeling ill at ease, didn't know what to say,
asked if we should go fishing together, but Knut didn't answer,
because one of his girls kept making a fuss about wanting to
go, let's go, they had to go. I was going out on the fjord to
fish that evening, I said. He could come if he wanted to. He
didn't answer, and that was what we both wanted. But it was
that evening, while I was out on the fjord, that the restlessness came over me. It was a lovely summer evening, it was
warm, light, with a cool wind, and I decided to take the boat

out on the fjord, do a bit of trolling. I get in the boat and I
decide to troll far enough out to see the house where Knut is
staying while he is here on holidays. Knut's father is dead,
there's just his mother left. She lives alone in the house. But
now Knut is there, he and his family. I am trolling past the
unpainted rundown old boathouse where Knut and I used
to play together when we were kids, and I can see the house
where Knut used to live, a white house, up on the hill a bit.
There's a path from the house down to the shore. Perhaps
Knut will see me, perhaps he'll come down, will want to
come fishing with me. But what should I say to him? He
mustn't come, it's all so long ago, and we don't have anything
to say to each other anymore. I look away quickly, increase
the speed, drive quickly past the house where Knut lives, and
then, with a sharp turn, I swing the boat around, away from
the shore, I push the small outboard motor as fast as it can go,
away from the shore, out on the fjord, and when I've reached
the middle of the fjord, I ease back, ease right back on the
speed, and then I reel in the trolling line, of course there
wouldn't be any fish out here, I hadn't expected that, just
wanted to get out and see if I could spot Knut, but I didn't
really want that either, I reel in the trolling line, rev up the
motor and set a new course, thinking I might head to the
small island where I usually fish, it's one of the best fishing
places around here, besides, it's a very nice spot, sheltered,
you can fish in peace, if you keep to the outside of the small
island no one can see you from land, and I think that's mostly
why I like fishing at the small island, I don't like people
watching me, have never liked it, and along the fjord there's

a narrow ploughed strip of land, with houses built on it. The houses face the fjord. There are people in the houses, and they might watch me. I sit at the back of the boat, the outboard motor is going at top speed, and I'm setting course toward the small island, I reach it, stop the motor, and start jigging, on the inside of the small island at first, I'm jigging, no bite, perhaps no fish to catch this evening. But it's a nice evening. I start feeling a hint of restlessness. I don't know what it is. Something has come over me, I don't know what it is, but I can feel a hint of restlessness. It's a nice evening. Mild, warm. I can feel a restlessness. A restlessness has come over me. I have never felt it before, and now I can see two boats further out on the fjord, lying still, I didn't see them when I arrived. There are two boats further out, a few meters from each other. The boats are lying still. I'm jigging. One of the boats is heading toward me. My restlessness grows. One of the boats is coming toward me. I keep jigging, I look the other way. My restlessness grows stronger. I don't want to turn around. I can hear by the sound of the outboard motor that the boat is coming closer. I have to turn around. I turn around, and I see her waving to me, I see Knut's wife, and she's waving to me, I see Knut's wife sitting at the back of a runabout, she's wearing a yellow rain jacket, I can see her face behind the hood, the black hair, the eyes, and she's waving to me, and she's coming closer, she slows down the speed of the outboard motor, she turns around to come alongside my boat, and she asks if I've caught any fish, and I don't know what to answer, the sky suddenly seems to have grown darker, and the rest-lessness has suddenly gone again, I catch my breath, best to get away, and why is she here now, alone in a runabout, I catch my breath, but my restlessness has disappeared, first I become restless, then calm, her boat's close, it has suddenly got dark, and I can see her taut thighs against the white oilcloth trousers she's wearing, and I turn my head away, turn away from her, and at that moment, I'd forgotten to jig the line, I'd kept the line completely still, I'd completely forgotten to jig, and at that moment I feel a tug and I give a start, a fish is biting, and I tell her I have a fish biting, I turn toward her, she brought fishing luck with her, I say, have to say something, talk about something ordinary, the fact she's here, have to say something, at first I get restless, without knowing why, and suddenly Knut's wife is in a boat alongside me, have to talk about something ordinary, I have a bite, the first bite today, and I've turned toward her, I think I'm smiling, and the fish's biting then, she says, and I turn away again, toward the rail, begin to pull in the line, slowly, steadily, I pull in the line, turn toward her, and she is so close to me, I have to say something, and I ask if she has caught anything, caught a fish, no, not even a bite, she says, and I say that perhaps the fish has gone to bed for the night. Have to say something. I pull. I grin. I see the fish, a nice good-sized cod. I'm careful, pull the fish right up to the rail, grasp the line well below the fish, I'm about to pull it over the rail, the fish is in the air, a nice cod that one, she says, and then. Then the cod splashes back into the water. There's the tail. There the fish swims, half a meter away, below the surface, just below, there he swings his tail. There the fish disappears downward, becomes invisible. I grin. I stand and look after the fish, it's gone, and I'm strangely relieved, I turn toward her, and I smile. She smiles at me. She has stopped her outboard motor, and her boat's drifting toward my boat, and I don't understand why my boat's not drifting too, my boat lies still. I look up, look toward land, and there, on the road, a few hundred meters up from the foreshore, there, on the road, I see Knut, I quickly look down again, he stands there quite still, he stands there almost stiff and looks toward us, he stands on the road and looks right at us. Her boat glides closer and closer to my boat, and now I can feel that she's really close to me, and I have to say something to her, can't just remain silent, have to tell her that Knut is standing on the shore, up there on the road, perhaps he wants to come with us, he too might want to fish. Her boat has drifted right up to my boat. Knut's looking down toward us.

You lost your fish, she says, and she's smiling at me.

It was a nice cod, too, I say.

At least there's fish here, she says, and she smiles.

Unless that one was the only one.

I should try my luck here too, for a while, she says, and she bends forward, I'm thinking I have to tell her that Knut's standing up there on the road, she picks up a fishing rod, and she stands up, lifts the rod, and with a clumsy movement, she is not very good at it, I'm thinking, but with a clumsy movement she lifts the rod up and backwards, throws it, and the spinner splashes into the water a couple of meters from her boat, and she sits down again, looks at me. She's sitting down now.

Not a very good throw, she says, and she laughs a little.

It takes practice to do it well, I say.

Yes, she says.

Silence.

Do you often go fishing? she asks.

Quite a lot in summer, I say.

You like it?

Yes.

Everything goes quiet again, and I turn around, turn away from her, take good care not to look toward land, because Knut's standing up on the road, standing there without moving, and he's looking toward us, and I turn away, I look down on the water. My restlessness has disappeared. I don't understand it. Her boat lies close to my boat. We are fishing.

Do you get a lot of fish then? she asks.

Well, now and then. When it bites I usually get a lot, I say.

What do you do with it?

My mother takes it off my hands.

You live with your mother?

Yes.

Have you lived in this place all your life?

Yes.

You don't go away anywhere?

I don't like going away.

Don't like going away . . .

Well, just a bit perhaps . . .

Why not?

Well, I say.

It doesn't matter, she says, and I look up, toward land,

and Knut is still standing there, it has gone very quiet, we are not talking anymore, and suddenly, she bends her head forward, bends her head toward me, and her rod tautens, I've got a bite, she shouts, she's got a bite now, a fish, come on, look at the rod, look how it bends all the way, she says, and she struggles with the rod, places it between her legs, wedges it under the seat and she starts reeling in the line, the rod keeps bending, she presses her lips together, and she keeps reeling in the fish, the rod keeps bending, it bends more and more, it bends as far as it can, and she gets up, she isn't very tall, she is small, she stands, leans forward, and she shouts that there's the fish, she can see him now, a nice cod, she says, and she reels in the line, the fish is in the air, is over the rail of the boat, is in the boat, and she pulls back a bit, stands there and looks at the fish, sits down. I can hear the fish flopping around in her boat, the tail beating rhythmically. I stand in my boat, looking at her catch.

Not a bad one, I say.

The biggest fish I've ever caught, she says.

Yes, it's a nice one, I say.

Fine fish, she says.

Not bad at all.

And it's a cod as well.

Yes.

What should I do with it? she asks.

You've got to bleed it, I tell her.

What's—

You can't leave the blood in the fish, it can destroy—

The fish is still alive.

Yes.

Couldn't you bleed it for me? she asks.

No problem, I tell her, and then I ask her to put the cod into the baler bucket she has in the boat, and she stands up, gets the bucket, tries to get the fish into it without touching it, finally she just prods the fish with one finger, it flails its tail, it flops around, it slides into the bucket, and she lifts up the bucket, stretches the hand that holds the bucket over the boat rail, her boat has drifted right up to my boat by now, and I stand up, take the bucket by the handle, grip the handle, well away from her hand, and then her hand slides toward mine, touches the skin of my hand, quickly, and then she pulls her hand away, I take the bucket into my boat, I should have told her that Knut is watching us from the road, she hasn't noticed him, mustn't look toward land, I think, and then I grab the fish by the gills with one hand, push the thumb on the other hand through the gill slits, tear it back, the fish wriggles, the blood spurts, and then I get a good grip through the mouth of the fish, hold it outside the boat and rinse it in the water, take it into the boat, lift the bucket over the boat rail, rinse it, and rinse off the blood on the boards with a bit of water. I put the fish into the bucket again and give it back to her, and this time, too, her hand slides over to mine, touches my skin, I grin to myself, but I've lost the sense of time, does she touch my hand for a long time, a short time, I'm not sure, but she gets the bucket, and I sit down again. Perhaps she touched my skin.

That looked disgusting, she says.

I'm used to it, I say.

She throws out the line again, and I want to ask why Knut isn't with her, tell her that he is watching us, but perhaps I oughtn't to, I think, perhaps it's rude to ask, she must've seen him herself, I think.

Is this small island your usual fishing place? she asks.

Yes, I say, and I look up, look toward land, and there, down on the foreshore, on a rock, there, right in front of me, on a rock on the foreshore, I see Knut, and he is throwing pebbles into the water. It must be Knut who is sitting there, and he is looking at the shore, at the sea, he is sitting there looking at us. Knut is sitting on the shore, he is looking at his wife, and his wife is alone in a rowboat, and that rowboat is lying close to my rowboat. I look down. I glance cautiously toward Knut's wife, but she is busy with her fishing. I look down at the sea. Knut is sitting on land, has to be Knut, I think. Knut's wife turns around, looks at me.

I think the fish has gone, she says.

I don't answer, don't look up.

There was probably only one in the first place. First you caught him, and when you lost him, he went for my hook.

Knut's wife smiles at me, and I look up warily, look warily toward land, the shore, the road, but her eyes don't follow the direction of my eyes, and Knut is still sitting there.

I should probably be getting back, I say, fumbling with my hands.

You've only just arrived here.

But the fishing isn't all that good.

I've been fishing for a while, she says.

I don't answer.

There's fish here, she says.

I look down into the boat.

Why don't you fish for a bit longer, it's nice to have company, she says.

I don't answer.

I'd like to go ashore on the small island, she says.

No, I say.

Yes, you want to, she says, and she stands up in the boat, reels in the line, sits down again, starts the outboard motor, and she's already on her way out to the small island, I can see her yellow rain jacket, can see the outboard motor, and I turn around, quickly, I turn, and I see Knut sitting on the rock on the foreshore, he's looking toward me, and I turn again, I start the outboard, have to get up speed quickly, have to tell her that Knut's sitting and waiting on the foreshore, must get up speed, I've got the outboard going, and I follow Knut's wife, she's steering toward the small island, slowing down, turning off the outboard motor, she moves to the front of the boat, stands there ready when she arrives at the shore, and I follow her, turn my boat alongside hers, turn off the motor, lift the propeller out of the water, turn off the fuel supply, move forward, grab the mooring rope and jump onto the shingled shore, and I look toward land, and Knut stands there still, he has stood up now, he stands there, on the foreshore, stands there motionless, and I climb over the rocky terrain, find a tree, sling the rope around the tree, and Knut's wife has sat down on a rock, she has pulled her knees up under her chin, her arms are folded around her legs, and I think that she must have seen Knut by now, her mooring rope is still lying next to her, and I go over to her, I say that I can tie her boat, I take the rope, I tie her boat, tie it to the tree that my boat is tied to. I grin. I look toward land, and Knut's standing there. Knut's wife looks at me, asks why I'm laughing. I say I'm not laughing. All right then, but I'm grinning. I ask if she wants to take a walk around the small island, just a short walk, and she nods, gets up, and I start walking across the rocks, up to the heather, almost the whole small island is covered in heather, there are lots of bushes, a few trees, a few rock formations, and on the other side, the side that faces outward, toward the fjord, where the fjord is at its widest, there, on the outside, there's a great cove. She walks behind me. I walk in front of her. She follows me, and she says I have to wait. I stop.

First time I'm on a small island, she says.

Yes, I say.

Do you come here often? she asks.

Almost never.

You've gone ashore here before?

Yes, I say, and we walk across the heather, I don't turn around, don't want to turn around, and she does not turn around either, she looks ahead of her, walks, doesn't want to turn around perhaps. I tell her that we can walk across to the cove, the best place on the whole small island, the cove is on the other side of the small island, the cove faces out toward the fjord, and she says yes, we could do that, she doesn't mind, it doesn't matter to her, she just wanted to go ashore on the small island, that's all. We walk across the small island, trample through the heather, drag ourselves up by the bushes, walk down toward the shore, follow the shoreline. For a short distance there is sand, a beach. She stops then, Knut's wife, and she makes a pattern in the sand with the tip of her shoe. I watch her. It's a nice summer evening, a soft evening, and Knut's wife is dressed for the rain, white oilcloth trousers, a yellow rain jacket. She has black hair and brown eyes. I've never talked to her before, and we walk along the shore, walk across some rocks, over a few hills covered in heather, and we can see the cove, I have to tell her now that Knut's standing on land, on the foreshore, I must tell her, I think. Knut's wife smiles at me.

You don't talk much, she says.

No.

Like most people from this place, she says.

I suppose.

I'm going to be here all summer, she says.

You've just arrived?

She says yes, and I feel a hint of intimacy, she said I, not we, and I have to tell her that Knut's standing there, on the shore, has been standing there for a long time, perhaps he wants to come with us, I don't know, must tell her.

Well, we arrived a couple of days ago, she says.

But you've been here before?

Oh yes, many times, she says.

Silence.

But I haven't seen you before, she says.

I stay at home most of the time.

You stay at home alone?

Yes, most of the time.

Why?

I don't know.

You should go out and meet people.

I shrug.

You prefer your own company then?

I suppose.

You're strange, she says.

Silence.

You're a funny guy, she says, and we have arrived at the cove, we sit down, we don't talk, we sit in total silence, it's just beginning to grow darker, the darkness is slowly falling, and I can't get the thought of Knut out of my head, Knut standing on the foreshore, at first he was standing on the road, then he walked down to the shore, he was just there, standing there motionless, I was careful not to meet his eyes, perhaps he noticed that I saw him, I don't know, and abruptly, out of the blue, and much stronger than earlier in the evening, and plain as day, the restlessness came over me, burrowed into my body, my left arm started to ache, my fingers, I'm aching, something has come over me, it gets darker, it grows steadily darker, and I look at Knut's wife, and she looks at me, and then I suddenly notice her eyes, and I know, suddenly I know, that I can't tell her that Knut's standing on the foreshore, I just can't tell her that, I don't know why, but I just can't. The restlessness is intense now, I have to get home, I decide, I tell her that, and she nods. We go back to the boats. I can't see Knut anymore. We start the outboard motors. I go first, and she follows behind me. On the fjord, going home. I look straight ahead, it is quiet, it has grown a little darker. The thundering of the outboard motors. Going home. And then I hear a shout. One shout. The restlessness. Never felt this restlessness before, and I hear a shout. I ease back on the speed, do a small turn. Knut's wife does the same. I look around, look toward land. Knut. On the headland, right behind us, I can see Knut, he stands there and waves, he shouts, asks if he can get a lift home. I turn the boat, set course for the point. Knut sits down on the point. He smiles, he saw us, he says, and he smiles. I don't know what to say. Knut's wife arrives in her boat and she says hi, good to see him.

I've caught a fish, she says.

Dinner tomorrow, says Knut.

A nice big cod, she says.

Let's have a look, says Knut, and he gets up, goes down to the water, and Knut's wife shows him the fish, it's a nice cod, he says, a good-sized cod, they'll cook it for dinner tomorrow, he says, nice with fish for dinner, he says, could salt down the fish tonight, have lightly-salted cod tomorrow, that'll be nice, fresh lightly-salted cod. Knut walks along the shore, over to my boat.

So did you catch anything then, he says, and he looks around in my boat.

I shake my head.

He caught a fish but he lost it again, she says.

Yes, I had him out of the water, almost to the rail of the boat, and then he fell in and disappeared, I say.

I suppose it was a hell of a big fish?

It was a nice big one, I say.

I'm sure it's the same fish I caught, Knut's wife says.

It was a cod too?

Yes, I say.

About the same size?

I nod.

We were fishing next to each other, first he caught a fish that he lost, and just afterward I caught a fish, she says.

Probably the same then, Knut says.

Cod don't swim in schools, I say.

You and the cod both, Knut says.

That wasn't very nice, Knut's wife says, and she laughs, and Knut says to me that first, we don't see each other for at least ten years, even if he has been here quite often, and then, suddenly, we meet twice in a day, and I nod, agree that yes, it's strange, and I don't know what to say, because Knut was standing on land, up on the road, he walked down to the foreshore, I saw him, and he saw me, saw that I saw him, and then Knut's wife and I went out to the small island. Knut was left on the shore. Then he shouts. When we are on our way back Knut's standing on the point shouting to us. I look at Knut, and he climbs into his wife's boat, goes to the outboard motor at the back of the boat, tells her to go and sit in the front of the boat. He starts the motor.

I suppose I should take her home, he says, turning toward me.

Yes, I say.

You always say yes, his wife says to me, and I nod, don't say anything, it's very strange this, and the restlessness, the intense restlessness, it's getting darker, and her eyes, her eyes are everywhere now, over the sky, over the fjord, and this restlessness, I have never noticed it before. Her eyes.

Well, we'd better be getting home, Knut says.

Good night then, I say, and the boat with Knut and his wife is already speeding away, speeding forward, outward, and I should start my own outboard motor, should follow, should get home. But I don't start the motor. I stay there, close to land, at the point, I must have been there for an hour, and the whole time I felt this restlessness, a restlessness I have never felt before, and then I start the outboard motor, I go out on the fjord, beyond the headland, stay there and fish, get quite a few fish now, the fishing's good, and then, when it was really dark, when the wind was freshening, I started the motor, went home. The whole time this restlessness was in me, this restlessness that suddenly had come over me, and her eyes were everywhere. She's Knut's wife. I go home, and now I sit here, every evening, I sit here and write. This restlessness won't let go of me. That's why I write. I have to get rid of this restlessness. This summer I met Knut again, I had not seen him for at least ten years, and a restlessness came over me. That is why I'm writing. I would like to get close to the restlessness, grab it by the neck and examine it. Knut and I were always together. Every day. Knut left, I called after him, but he just left. I met Knut's wife. It was the same day I saw Knut again. I had not seen Knut for at least ten years, and now he was married, had two kids. Knut is dancing with someone from our class. That was the day the restlessness came over me, and since then it has just grown more and more intense. Knut's wife. I sit here and write, have to keep the restlessness at bay. A yellow rain jacket. I don't go out any longer. My mother.

A restlessness has come over me. I don't go out any longer. It was this summer that the restlessness came over me. That is why I write. Knut's wife, a yellow rain jacket, the denim jacket. My mother is walking around on the floor below me. She watches television, goes shopping. My mother. She does the shopping. I used to do the shopping, now I don't go out anymore. It was this summer that the restlessness came over me, and since then I have not gone out. My mother is not all that old. I met Knut again, and I watched him leave, watched his back leaving. Knut left. I called after him. I don't know. It's this restlessness. I haven't touched the guitar since the restlessness came over me, and I don't go out. What's wrong with you, my mother says. You can't just sit inside, she says. It was this summer that I met Knut again, he had got married, had two kids. It's this restlessness, I don't know, but this restlessness. I called to Knut, but he didn't answer, he just left. I haven't seen him again since then. I have to keep the restlessness at bay, that's why I write. It was this summer that the restlessness came over me. I don't go out anymore. I haven't touched my guitar since the restlessness came over me, I don't play my records any longer. My left arm aches, my fingers. My mother. Knut's wife. A yellow rain jacket. The denim jacket. Her eyes. A restlessness has come over me and

I write. The guitar. I can see my guitar. I remember my first guitar. Knut and I. This summer I met Knut again, and it was then this restlessness came over me. Knut had got married, had two kids. When we were kids, Knut and I were always together. Every day. As we were growing older we were always together too. It was Knut and I who started to play in a band together. Knut and I decided to start a band, a rock band, and I don't know how old we were, eleven years, perhaps, and during a recess at school Knut and I decided to start a rock band, and during recess we keep to ourselves, walk around planning, at first we thought there had to be more of us, had to be four of us because in our band there had to be two guitars, electric guitars, of course, and then there had to be a bass and percussion, and then one of us had to sing, or perhaps we should have someone who could just be the vocalist, in any case we had to have a microphone, then we had to have speakers, with amplifiers, a microphone stand, cables, we had to have all that, and then we had to have song lyrics, we'd need somewhere to practice as well, but to begin with we could probably practice in our boathouse, as we called it, and a name, the band had to be called something. Knut and I planned and planned. Knut and I tell each other that we're going to be really good, going to play at dances everywhere. I would really like to play the guitar, Knut wants to as well. Going home that day. Knut and I riding our bikes side by side. Riding side by side on our bikes, and at the Youth Club Knut suddenly braked and swung his bike toward the deck in front of the entrance, threw his bike aside, and leapt up the stairs to the entrance door. Here, he said. We could practice here. Can't see why not. We could practice in the Youth Club. Well we had to practice somewhere, that was important, he said. And there's no electricity in the boathouse, and we had to have that, he said. I agreed, and we decided to ask there and then, one of the shop assistants at The Co-op was the chairman of the Youth Club, Knut knew that, so we could ride the bikes to The Co-op right now, could ask the chairman of the Youth Club right now, and that's what we did, we threw ourselves on our bikes, cycling inland at a furious pace, along the road, up the hills, standing on those pedals down the slopes, going inland, inland toward The Co-op, up the last slope, turning into the entrance to the shop, getting off the bikes, putting the bikes into the bike racks, into the shop, asking for the chairman of the Youth Club, and he's down at the wharf, that's where he usually is, the woman at the cash register said and we ran down the stairs, down to the wharf, and there he was, the chairman of the Youth Club, and we asked if we could practice in the Youth Club, we were going to start an orchestra, we said, at first we called it an orchestra, not a band, and could we practice in the Youth Club, we needed somewhere to practice, couldn't practice at home, we'd be using amplifiers and percussion, there'd be a lot of noise, and so we couldn't practice at someone's place, and the shop assistant grinned, looked at us, asked if our parents agreed to this, if we knew how to play, if we had all the equipment we needed, and then, yes, then it might be possible to practice in the Youth Club, he thought it could be possible, but he didn't make all the decisions on his own, yes, he was the chairman, but he couldn't make all the decisions, not on his own, if we actually could play, well, he would put it to the board, yes he would, and something could be worked out, he thought. He grinned. Knut and I winked furiously to each other, nodded. And the shop assistant was standing there grinning. But did we have any equipment? We said that we didn't have anything quite yet. The chairman of the Youth Club said we almost certainly could practice in the Youth Club hall, that shouldn't be any problem, he said. What about the equipment? It was expensive to buy musical equipment, and did we know how to play? Knut said, all right, we didn't have any equipment yet, but you have to start somewhere, and we didn't know how to play either, but at one stage you've got to start learning that, too, he said. The chairman of the Youth Club agreed with that. Besides, Knut said, today was the day we were going to start getting our equipment together. Then the shop assistant said that he might be able to help us with some of that. Because in the storeroom he'd seen an old microphone stand, it looked exactly like a microphone stand, exactly like it, you could mistake it for one, a few iron spikes had been hanging from it, just like an umbrella, the spikes were to hang merchandise on, but they didn't use this display stand anymore, and he thought we could have it, if we wanted it. He was already on his way into the storeroom, and we followed him. Knut and I walked behind the shop assistant, and we winked furiously to each other. Nodded to each other. The shop assistant climbed over a few pallets with sacks of flour, disappeared behind there somewhere, and then a shiny iron rod appeared, more and more of it came into view, a long iron rod, then we saw a black foot, it looked like a Christmas tree foot, except this was black, then we saw the chairman's hand, and then the whole chairman. This should do the job, he says, and we stand there dumbstruck, it would certainly do the job, it's like a proper microphone stand, all we need to do is cut the rod, it's far too long, and of course the shop assistant had to say that since we were so small and since the rod was so long, one of us could stand on the shoulders of the other one, and then sing out loud, as he said, and then he laughed. We would fill the Youth Club to the rafters if we performed that way, he said. We didn't think it was particularly funny. But the rod was put down on the floor, and it really looked like a proper microphone stand. And now all that's missing is a microphone, the shop assistant said. Actually, there was a microphone in the Youth Club, but it didn't work. And there was an amplifier, too, and that worked, and there were a couple of speakers, and they should work. He thought we'd be able to borrow the equipment for the time being. We stood there, just nodding, good, we said, and, thanks a lot, and then we took the microphone stand with us, one of us held the foot, that was me, the other held the rod from the top end, that was Knut, and with the microphone stand between us, we walked up the stairs, up toward the shop. Far out, talk about being lucky, said Knut. Not only had we gotten ourselves a place to practice, we'd gotten ourselves a microphone stand, we'd gotten hold of an amplifier and two speakers. We'd managed to get all this in one day. Far out, he said. Our bikes were still outside the shop, with our schoolbags on the luggage rack. Problem, said

Knut. We couldn't manage both the bikes and the rod, he thought. No, probably not, I said. So we'll have to leave the bikes, we'll have to come back for them later, and first get the microphone stand home and housed, Knut thought, and no doubt he was right. So we start walking up the road, first Knut and then me, carrying the microphone stand between us, and we decide to carry it out to the boathouse, that's the best place, we agree, and if we don't get another place to practice, we could practice there, we both agree, we could at least start there, we tell each other. We walk up the road. We carry the microphone stand between us. But can we go straight to the boathouse just like that, I wonder. None of us owns the boathouse, I say. We've just been playing there a lot. We stop. Knut looks at me. He nods. We'll walk to the foreshore first, get to the boathouse from the foreshore, the way we usually go, he says. I nod. Then we start walking again, we walk over to the other side of the road, we look around, can someone see us, we can't see anyone, and then we walk to the edge of the road, over to a hill, and then we walk down toward the foreshore, it's very steep but we walk slowly, keep our balance, almost fall a couple of times, but we manage to get down to the foreshore. Then Knut says that perhaps we should rest for a bit, I nod, and we sit down on a couple of rocks. We sit in silence. Look out over the fjord. We pick up a pebble each, throw it into the sea, not very far, just so it falls into the sea. This is going really well, Knut says. Can't believe it, I say. The microphone stand lies between us, on the rocks and pebbles on the shore. Bloody great guy, that chairman of the Youth Club, I say. Yes far out, Knut says. We sit on our rocks, throw pebbles into the sea, and then we look at each other, we get up, grab an end each of the microphone stand, and then we start walking along the foreshore. Knut and I walk along the foreshore, Knut walks first, I walk behind him, and between us we carry an old display stand from The Co-op, but it looks exactly like a microphone stand. Knut and I walk along the foreshore, now we pass below Svein on Leite's farm, he owns the boathouse were heading toward, so I tell Knut that we shouldn't talk too loudly, at least not about where were heading, and Knut nods, agrees. We walk along the foreshore, we don't talk. Suddenly Knut stops, and I turn around, look at him, and Knut nods toward the fruit trees of Svein of Leite's farm. I look up there, where the branches are laden with apples and pears. The fruit looks nice. Knut and I stand still, then we say that first of all we have to get the microphone stand home and housed, and later, perhaps, we could, and Knut nods, we start walking again. I can hear the waves crashing and rolling against the shore. I can see the boathouse. I can hear the waves. We walk toward the boathouse. I try to walk in time with the rolling waves. Knut and I walk toward the boathouse. We arrive, we walk along the side of the boathouse, there's a small door there, not much more than a hatch, that we mostly use. The hatch is only fastened on the outside with a hook. I take the hook off, open the hatch, crawl in, and Knut hands me the microphone stand. It's dark inside the boathouse. It has an earthen floor. Knut comes in, and he pulls the hatch back in place. We stand there for a while without moving, have to let our eyes get used to the dark, and when we're able to distin-

guish dim shapes Knut places himself in front of the microphone stand, then I join him, and we realize it's far too long,
and Knut says we've got to cut it off if we're going to use it,
and then we decide to do just that, to do it right away, we
decide, but we mustn't cut too much, then it'll be too short
before you know it, we warn each other. But if we're going to
cut it we have to go home to his place or to my place to get
a hacksaw, and we decide to go home to my place, as that's
the closest. We should do it at once, we decide, but first we
have to hide the microphone stand, we tell each other, and
we look around, where can we put it, and we decide to put it
under a half-rotten rowboat that's lying overturned on the
floor, along one of the walls, and we manage to do it, the rod
itself slides easily under the boat, but the foot of the stand is
a problem, but we get it almost under the boat. And then we
walk outside again. Push up the hatch, stand outside. The
light is so strong it hurts our eyes. Knut and I trot up to the
main road, along the road, up to my place, down to the
basement, and we find a hacksaw, and when we are on our
way out of the basement again of course my mother is on her
way down there, she has been waiting for me, she says, I'm
very late, she says, and where's my schoolbag, my bike, and I
tell her about the band we're going to start, about my
schoolbag, I'm on my way to fetch my schoolbag now, I tell
her, it's on my bike outside The Co-op, I'm going to get it
immediately, I tell her, and she says that my dinner is cold by
now, and I say that's fine, no problem, I can eat cold food, I
tell her, and she is about to say something else, but Knut and
I are already on our way down to the main road, turning into

it. We're making plans, first he has to go home, at once, or he'll get an earful, and then he'll come back to my place, and we'll go down to the boathouse, where we'll cut the microphone stand. That's what we have to do. We walk to The Co-op, and our bikes are still there, our school bags are on the bike racks, and we get on our bikes, hurry home, and down the road we see Svein of Leite come walking toward us, walking right toward us, he takes up almost the whole road, he has almost killed kids who have stolen his pears, and talk about being a busybody, he has to know everything, now he's going to ask us about the microphone stand, Knut says, and Svein of Leite puts his hand out, tells us to stop, says he saw us walking down on the foreshore carrying something or other, what was that, he wonders, and Knut tells him it was nothing in particular, and Svein of Leite says it certainly was, he'd never seen anything quite like it before, and he's lived here for a long time, he's an old man, has lived here his whole life, and he has never seen anything quite like that thing before, and then Knut says, his voice a bit proud, that it was a microphone stand, and then Knut pushes down hard on the pedals, and I ride after him, and behind us we hear Svein of Leite ask what on earth do we want with a microphone stand, we're going to use it for something, Knut shouts, and we push those pedals as hard as we can, whisper to each other that Svein of Leite has seen us after all, perhaps he saw us go down to his boathouse, too, damn, Knut says, and I don't answer, I'm sure that Svein of Leite didn't see us, couldn't have seen us, I think, and then Knut and I say see you later to each other, agree that we've got to talk, I hurry home, my mother isn't angry with me, just says that she gets worried about me when I don't come straight home from school, you never know, she says, I eat my dinner, go outside, find the hacksaw, I'd put it on the basement steps, sit down on the garden bench to wait, kick my legs, dangle the saw, wait, and then I see Knut, he comes trotting down the road, he waves at me, I wave back, I stand up, run down to the main road, meet Knut, we smile at each other, discuss sawing off the stand, how to make it the right height, but first we have to find something that could pose as a microphone, Knut says, and we decide to go down to the foreshore, we should be able to find something there, and we run down to the foreshore, we walk, we potter around in the pebbly sand, find bits of driftwood, sticks, tin cans, empty plastic bottles, we are walking along the foreshore when Knut has the idea that perhaps we should sing a song, we stop, look at each other, neither of us dare to start, so we keep walking, but really, we should sing a song, we have to know one song at least, a few songs, and I keep thinking, actually, I don't know any songs, only songs for children. We walk on the pebbles and the gritty sand. It's early autumn, the weather's mild, the sea is breaking gently against the shore. The trees are in autumn colors. There is fruit on the trees. We are on the foreshore below Svein of Leite's farm. The man who laughed so terribly at us today. Svein of Leite has a lot of fruit. Many pear trees, terrific apples. An apple would taste great just now, or perhaps a pear. A pear would taste even better. We look up toward the farm. The trees closest to us are pear trees. So a pear would taste great. We look quickly at each other, and decide at once. We walk up to the edge between the farm and the shore, and then we run, as fast as we can, from the shore up the hill toward Svein of Leite's farm, run fast, bent double, hurrying up to the closest tree, and, straightening up, we take a good look around, stretch our hands up in the air, get hold of a pear each, first one, then another, we put the pears in the pockets of our pants, as many as we can stuff into the pockets, and then we bend down again, heads down, bodies bent double, and with small steps we trot down to the shore. We find a couple of rocks a bit further down on the foreshore, sit on a rock each, and start munching on the pears. We eat one pear, then another. We're munching on the pears. Throwing the cores in the water. There, Knut suddenly says. Look over there, he says. It looks like a microphone, he says, and he gets up, and munching on his pear he runs over and picks up a piece of brown driftwood. It really looks like a microphone. He picks up the piece of timber, holds it in front of his mouth, and says something in a language that sounds a bit like English. Knut runs the fingers on his other hand through his hair, and then he bends his neck forward, pushes his lips out, presses the piece of timber hard against his lips, holds one fist tight around the microphone and the other up in the air, and then he sings. In a loud voice. Knut stands on the foreshore, below Svein of Leite's farm, and sings. Knut sings in a loud voice. He sings in a language that sounds a bit like English. I tell him not to sing so loud or Svein of Leite's sure to come, and Knut goes silent, sits down on the rock, fishes another pear out of his pocket, munches on it, and then we decide it's time to get back to the boathouse

again, and we walk along the foreshore, listen to the waves, I
walk to the rhythm of the waves, the hacksaw dangling from
my hand, the tide is coming in, the sea is much closer to the
shore now than when we walked here earlier, we walk over
to the boathouse, our pockets full of pears, we walk along
the side of the boathouse, climb in through the hatch, me
first, then Knut, and when we are inside we hurry over to the
overturned rowboat, get down on our knees, pull the microphone stand from its hiding place beneath the overturned
rowboat, stand it upright, stand in front of it, decide where
to cut it, we want to have it about eye-level, we decide, and
then we start sawing, that takes time, but we persevere, and
when we have finished, Knut holds the piece of timber on
top of the microphone stand, and it looks just like the proper
thing, like it should look, it looks almost like the proper
thing. We should've had guitars too, I point out, and Knut
nods. It is dark in the boathouse, it smells musty. Knut stands
behind the microphone stand, and I look at him. Knut twists
his head back and forth and moves his lips. But not a sound
comes out of his mouth. I stand in front of him, and I too
twist my head back and forth. We keep this up for a while,
until Knut looks at me, and I look at him, and then, without
the need to say a word, we look toward the ladder that leads
up to the loft in the boathouse, nod to each other, leave the
microphone stand where it is and we run toward the ladder,
first Knut, then me, then I see Knut climbing up, then I start
to climb. We're up on the loft. We look at our table, two
herring crates set on top of each other. Two candle stumps
are waxed onto the table. A box of matches lies next to them.

Knut goes and lights one of the candles. There's more natural light up here on the loft, the light comes from a small skylight under the roof. Then Knut stiffens, looks at me with big round eyes, and he holds his finger in front of his mouth, whispers, shush. I stand stock-still. It's probably nothing, says Knut, but I thought I could hear something, he says, and then he goes and sits down on the two herring crates, and I ask if he really wants to sit on the table, you can't do that, I say, but Knut doesn't answer, just keeps staring into thin air with an important look on his face, and then I walk over too, sit down next to Knut, one of the candles is spluttering between us, and we sit quietly, without talking. This has been our lucky day, I say. Yes, far out, says Knut. I think we're actually going to make it happen, this band, I say, and Knut nods. I think so too, he says. Then we start fishing the pears out of our pockets, we put them on the table, next to the two candle stumps. We should really have a bench up here, I say. Just what I was thinking, says Knut. We often think the same thing, I say. Knut nods. And then, about the same time, we think about the fact that there are some old fishing nets in the shed, and some old empty flour sacks, and then it's obvious what we can do, it's not a problem to make a bench. But we've got to speak in a whisper, says Knut, he's sure he heard something up on the road. Perhaps it was Svein of Leite, he had spoken to us earlier today, had seen us walking down on the foreshore, perhaps it was him Knut had heard up on the road. He'd heard something, that was for sure, said Knut. Svein of Leite didn't use his boathouse, but what if he suddenly decided to use it, Knut said, but if he came here, well, we were ready for him, and then we decided to pretend that he came, it was Knut who thought about that, and I agreed, and so, we both got up at once and Knut hurried over to one corner, there was an empty barrel there, and he climbed into it, and I ran over to the other corner, where a herring crate stood on its end, and I hid behind it, and then neither of us moved, and neither of us said a word. I thought it was getting a bit creepy, thought I could hear someone coming up the ladder. After a while I heard Knut's voice saying that no one seemed to be coming after all, and I said no, no one seemed to be coming, this boathouse is just standing here, I said, and then I came out from my hiding place, and I watched Knut come crawling out of the barrel, he was dusty and grimy, and Knut looked at me, said far out, it's really dark inside a barrel, and then we just stand there, stand there and look at each other, and once more I watch as Knut raises his eyebrows, stands stock-still, looks at me, but after a while he just shakes his head lightly, and he says it's nothing after all, today he thinks he can hear sounds everywhere, he says, and so we walk across the timber floor, and it gives under us as we walk, and we walk over to the ladder, climb down, first Knut then I, and then we are down in the darkness once more, and Knut says we forgot to blow out the candle, and I nod, but Knut says it doesn't matter, we're soon going back up again, he says, and then Knut goes and opens the hatch, and a square beam of light cuts dimly through the dusty air. The light beam hits the microphone stand, and Knut and I look at each other, tell each other it looks great, far out, says Knut, and I nod. The microphone stand is in the middle of the light beam. On the floor next to the microphone stand lays the hacksaw. A stack of herring crates are piled up against one wall. An old half-rotten rowboat lies overturned along the other wall. From the ceiling hangs an old half-rotten cotton net. A crate full of empty liquor bottles stands against the wall, next to the overturned boat. Knut looks around, and then he says, what we've got to do if we're going to make a bench, and that is what we're going to do, isn't it, we've got to tear strips off the net, a whole big pile, and then we've got to stuff the strips into one of the flour sacks. Knut looks at me, and I nod, and then we go for it, we start tearing strips off the net, we keep tearing, and a pile of torn strips from the net is beginning to form on the floor, and we decide we'll first tear off a pile, then carry it up, then tear again, then carry. We keep tearing. There's a pile of torn strips from the net on the floor, next to the microphone stand, and Knut says that I should keep tearing and he'll start carrying, and then Knut takes an armful of torn strips, climbs up, while I keep tearing, it's very dusty, but the pile on the floor gets bigger and bigger. In the middle of the light beam from the open side hatch is the microphone stand. The dust is very visible in the light. I tear more strips, glance at the microphone stand, and Knut comes down again, says that the candle has gone out by itself, which is funny, he says, and Knut bends down, takes a new bundle of torn strips, goes toward the ladder, while I keep tearing more strips off the net and looking at the microphone stand, and Knut comes back down, stops in front of the microphone stand and says far out, hey, it looks like the proper thing, that microphone stand, he says, far out, then he looks

at the pile of torn net strips at my feet, says that it's probably
enough now, should be sufficient, that's exactly the word he
uses, sufficient, should be sufficient to make a good bench, so
we should bring a flour sack up with us, stuff it with the
strips from the net, says Knut, and he looks at me, I nod, I'm
really pretty tired of standing there and tearing strips off the
net, so I say yes, that's got to be enough, and then Knut picks
up the pile with strips of torn net, says can I bring the flour
sack, and then we climb the ladder again, as always Knut
goes first, I go second, and when I get upstairs I see a big pile
of torn strips on the timber floor, and I say we've sure torn
up a lot of net, and Knut nods, a whole lot, yes, he says, it'll
be a good bench, he says, and points to the pile, and then I
hear, this time I can hear it properly, and without doubt, this
time someone is walking outside, no doubt about it, and I
look at Knut, he looks at me, we don't move, look into each
other's eyes, look down, don't move, we can both hear
someone walking outside, heavy steps, and then we hear
someone saying, in a strong voice, Svein of Leite's voice
saying why, the side hatch is open, well, he'll have to get it to
shut properly, he says, and Knut and I look at each other, and
I can see that Knut's face changes a little, his jaws tighten just
a little, and then I hear feet dragging through the grass, hear
a throat being cleared, then I hear the hatch banging against
the wall, hear the scraping of iron against iron, it's the hook
being fastened, I look at Knut, I see he's trying all he can to
hold his lips straight, then I hear Svein of Leite telling
himself it's really strange, he hasn't been in the boathouse for
ages, can't remember the last time he was here, the door had

probably got loose somehow, he says, and then I hear Svein of Leite shuffle off, I look at Knut, his eyes are big, they are a bit damp, he looks at me, he is silent, then he looks down, straight down, and I realize I have to say something, and suddenly I know what to say, I look at Knut, I say, Knut, it'll be all right, we can just use the other door, it can be opened from inside, there's a beam across it, and we can just take that off, right Knut, I say, the double doors where they drag the boats out, I say, and Knut looks up, nods, smart, he says, of course, he says, and then Knut is already on his way to the ladder, he climbs down, I turn, check that the candle is out, it is, and then I climb down too, I say we should hang on, he's not exactly fast on his feet, Svein of Leite, mustn't see us coming out of the boathouse, I say, and we walk over to the microphone stand, place ourselves behind it, stand there straight up and down, I think we're actually going to make it happen, this band, I say, and Knut nods, then he says that I mustn't forget to take the hacksaw home, I pick up the saw, then we walk over to the double doors, grab the beam that lies across the door from one end each, heave, it's heavy, we heave again, pressing our shoulders hard against the wall, the beam is loosening, we heave again, the beam is loosening now, sliding out of its brackets, we remove it, open the door, and we're blinded by brilliant light. We go outside. We decide to open the side hatch again, we go inside, put the beam back in place behind the double doors, go out through the hatch. That's what we do. We walk up to the main road, and Knut says that he should be getting home, we can talk more about our rock band at school tomorrow, we've already made a start, he really thinks we have, Knut says, have got ourselves a proper microphone stand and everything, he says, and we can practice in the Youth Hall, in the beginning perhaps we could just as well practice in the boathouse, he says, and I say all right we'll talk tomorrow then, yep alright says Knut, tomorrow, we'll have to go back to the boathouse again tomorrow, I say, have a look at the microphone stand, and the bench, we totally forgot that when Svein of Leite came, I say, so we did, says Knut, we'll have to finish it tomorrow, says Knut, and we've got the pears there too, but tomorrow, I say, it's good for them to be left overnight, they'll ripen, and then we say see you later one more time, and Knut walks along the road, right on the edge of the road, and I walk the other way, home to my place, and wonder if I would meet Svein of Leite, but I don't meet him. I'm thinking that we're going to have a really good band. I walk home. This summer I met Knut again. He has become a music teacher, has got married, has two kids. That's how it started. My life hasn't amounted to much, and now I sit here, every evening, and I'm scared, a restlessness has come over me. I don't know why I suffer from this restlessness. It's because of this restlessness that I write. Knut and I, we started a rock band together. That's a long time ago. This summer I met Knut again. It was then this restlessness came over me. I have decided to write, and now I sit here and write, every day, every evening. I'm over thirty years old, no job, no education. This is how it started, with a local rock band that got as far as playing at a few dances. I just sit here. I'm scared, my left arm aches, my fingers ache. This summer I met Knut again. Knut's wife. Her eyes. The denim jacket. I sit here, every evening, in the attic of an older white house, downstairs is the living room, and the kitchen, a bedroom where my mother sleeps, and I live up here, in the attic. I don't go out anymore, that's why I write, not for any other reason. I refuse to take any notice of the ache in my left arm, the ache in my fingers. This summer I met Knut again. I watch Knut dance with someone he used to go to school with. Hadn't seen him for many years. He has gotten married, has two kids. Has become a music teacher. And I haven't made much of my life. Knut left, and I called after him, and he just left. I just sit here. My mother is walking across the floor below me. I haven't made much of my life. Knut and I decided to start a band. In a recess we decided we should do that. We got two others to join us. That's how it all started. We managed to get instruments and equipment. Knut just left, I was watching his back, but he just left. This summer I met Knut again.

I hear my mother walking across the floor below me. I hear the sound of the television set. I sit and write. I don't go out anymore. I am restless, and I write. I haven't made much of my life. And this summer I met Knut again, he has become a music teacher. Knut's wife. Not much is happening with me, I'm unemployed, no income, not much of anything, really. I even live in a pretty isolated spot, in a small country village. I'd been restless for a long time when I began to write. Now I write every day. It was this summer, out on the fjord, when I was fishing, with Knut's wife, it was then the restlessness came over me. I met Knut again, I hadn't seen him for many years, and the same evening, out on the fjord, a fine summer evening, a mild evening, Knut's wife is also fishing, I can hear an outboard motor coming closer, and it's Knut's wife, she stops the motor, maneuvers her boat close to mine, and I can see Knut standing there on land, at least I think I see him, but perhaps he wasn't there after all, perhaps it was just me who thought I saw him, I don't know. But in any case he was standing on the headland calling out to us when we were going home. That's a fact. Now it's getting late, my mother has gone to bed, she called up to me that she was going to bed, and don't you sit up too late, she said. I sit here and write. And this summer I met Knut again. We used to be

together all the time. But that's a long time ago, it must be
at least ten years. Knut has become a music teacher, has got
married, has a family. Knut's wife. I met his wife the evening
after the fishing trip, too. That was just a coincidence. I
was only going for an evening walk, was walking along the
road. Past the house where Knut and his family were staying
during the holidays. There were lights on in every room. That
was unusual, during winter Knut's mother spent much of her
time in the kitchen, it's an old house, difficult to heat, so she
kept to the kitchen, either there or the bedroom at the other
end of the house. Now the whole house was lit up. It was
early evening, and I was walking along the road. I walked past
the house where Knut and his family were staying during
the holidays, walked outward for a while, turned around and
walked inland again. Then I see Knut's wife coming toward
me. She's wearing a denim jacket. I just keep walking along
the road. She looks at me, smiles, lifts a hand. We meet. I
stop. She's walking on the side of the road.
     Good to see you again, she says.
     Yes, I say.
     The cod was good.
     Yes, I'm sure it was, I say.
     Haven't had such a nice fish for dinner for a long time.
     No.
     Perhaps you're not all that fond of fish?
     Not very.
     But you like to fish, she says, and she's laughing at me and
just remains standing there on the side of the road, I don't
really know what to say now.

Well, I'm sure you do, she says.

Fishing's all right, I say.

She laughs. I just stand there and I don't know what to say, I don't know what to do with my hands, I don't know where to look.

Are you going out on the fjord tonight too? she asks.

I don't know, I say.

You'll think about it, she says, and she laughs again, stands there on the side of the road and laughs. She laughs with her whole body.

Perhaps we can go fishing, you and me, she says.

Yes, I say.

Knut's not all that keen on fishing.

He never was, I say.

But you've been fishing all your life?

I look at her.

Have you? she asks.

In summer at least.

And you don't eat fish.

That's not the point.

It's being out on the fjord.

I nod. I can see a car coming, and the thought occurs to me that it's probably not a good idea to stand here, to stand on the side of the road, stand and talk to Knut's wife, and she says that there's a fair bit of traffic here, she'd thought the village was so isolated that there wouldn't be much traffic, but there are cars on the road almost all the time, she says, standing on the side of the road, she stands there with her eyes, with her blue denim jacket, and she smiles, she's a little different from yesterday, I think, she's almost not quite the same person, this is the third time I see her, and now she seems totally different from the first time I met her, over there, a bit further down the road, just opposite the boathouse where Knut and I used to play when we were kids, where she gave me her hand, carefully offering it to me, when she said it was a pity it never made a record, that orchestra we used to play in, that time, long ago, and out on the fjord she was different too, difficult to describe how she was out there, and now, this time, now there's something else again, as she stands there on the side of the road, small, a bit plump, with black hair, thick hair, with her eyes, there she stands on the side of the road laughing, and she asks if we can go fishing together, and there isn't only one car passing, there are two cars behind that one again, and we stand next to each other on the side of the road. The cars pass. She walks into the road.

And Knut, I say.

He's putting the kids to bed, she says.

I nod.

Why don't you come up, say hello to Knut.

I hesitate, don't answer, it's been so long since Knut and I saw each other, we don't really have anything to say to each other, haven't found anything to say so far, it's all so long ago, so many years have passed, he has become a music teacher, has gotten married, is here on holidays, has brought two daughters, and I have just stayed here, haven't managed to get away, not managed to do anything, and Knut's wife, she stands there and asks me to come inside, to say hi to Knut, as she calls it. Knut. I stand on the side of the road.

Of course you must come, she says.

Perhaps, I say.

No you must, she says.

Are you going home now? I ask.

Yes.

But—

I was just going out for some fresh air, she says.

Oh I see.

I suppose I should come then.

Knut'll be pleased, she says, and she has already started to walk along the road, she walks in front of me, not very far to walk before we get to the road that leads up to Knut's house, we walk along the main road, she in front, I follow a little behind, all the times Knut and I used to ride our bikes like this, he in front, and me following a little behind, and then he would turn onto his road, look around, and standing on the pedals, he would ride up the hill, turn and shout see you later or see you soon, see you in the boathouse, for practice, see you, we were always going to see each other, and now Knut's wife is walking up the road, up to Knut's place, she walks a little ahead of me, it's a fine summer's evening, light, a fine evening, and I follow her, a little timidly, I'm dreading it, sitting in the same room as Knut, and I won't know what to say, have never known what to say, I don't know now either, walking behind Knut's wife, a little behind her, walking behind her because she knows I won't talk anyway, that I'm just walking, saying yes, no, perhaps, saying nothing because I have nothing to say, haven't got anything to say, always have some strange feeling or other, but almost never thoughts, have never got anything to say, there's nothing to talk about, just this strange feeling, and it always changes, and there's nothing you can say about that, and Knut's wife walks up the stairs to the porch, and I've often been on this porch, I can't count the times I've walked up these stairs, knocked on the door, asked for Knut, asked if Knut's at home if his mother or his father or one of his sisters or brothers opened the door. Perhaps Knut did. It was usually Knut. Knut knew when I was coming. We had arranged it, either earlier in the day or the day before. He would open the door and stand there. And then something would happen. On its own. Just like that. There was always something to talk about. Conversation never ran out. Knut's wife opens the door and walks into the hall, the door's open, I follow, I bend down on the porch, untie my shoelaces, and one of Knut's girls comes running down the stairs, calling hi mum, you're home already, we thought you'd be out for a lot longer, and there's something strange in the way the girl says it, as if she's a little scared or has been a little scared, perhaps it's not like that, but the girl stands close to her mother while I get my shoes off and walk into the main hall.

Look who I've brought with me, she says to the girl.

The man we met yesterday, the girl says.

The other girl I saw yesterday, she's a bit younger, she too comes down the stairs, but slowly, holding on to the banister, walking carefully down the stairs, step by step. I'm standing in the hall in Knut's house, and I don't know what to do with myself, do with my arms, with my hands, I'm just standing there. And then I hear Knut's wife call out to Knut, and he answers, and the answer comes from upstairs, he answers what is it this time, is he never to have any peace, and then she says he must come down, he has a visitor, and after a while I see Knut coming down the stairs, his hair's disheveled, as if he has been asleep, and he's wearing a pair of old slippers. When he sees me standing there in the hall, with no shoes, but still wearing my coat, he smiles, blinks his eyes, and he tucks one shirttail back into his trousers.

Good to see you, he says.

I just stand there.

I picked him up down on the road, she says, turning to Knut.

I grin with my nose.

She knows what she wants, that one, Knut says, turning to me while he nods his head toward his wife. I just stand there, and Knut's wife asks if I'm going to take off my jacket, I nod, take off my jacket, she comes with a clothes hanger, takes the jacket from me, and I notice, as I'm standing there in the hall, I notice the old smell that Knut's house used to have, that smell's still there, a special smell, no other house ever smelled like Knut's house, even if every house that the same people have lived in for a long time has its own special smell, there's this smell in Knut's house, the smell I knew almost every day for so many years, and now, it's ten years since I have seen Knut, and I can't have been in this house for about fifteen years, not since Knut moved out, not since he went away to go to senior high school, then I stopped going to his house, of course we were together when he came home, we practiced, still had our band then, but I stopped coming to his house, but now, for the first time, for the first time in

what must have been fifteen years, I'm once more standing in
the hall in Knut's house, and Knut's standing on the last step
of the stairs, the stairs leading up to the attic, the stairs to the
attic where Knut had his room, I watch Knut standing on
the stairs, and I feel that he too is so different from yesterday,
I feel that everything has changed, it's as if Knut was one
person when I met him on the road, when I saw him coming
around the bend, when I saw him again by accident after all
these years, and he was a completely different person when
he stood there on the headland, and his wife said he was
nasty when he said something to me, I can't even remember
what he said, and now he's standing there, standing on the
stairs, and he's almost like he used to be, in the old days, and
he asks me to come in, must come into the living room, and
he goes in first, then his wife, I remain standing where I am
for a while, the two girls remain standing there, too, looking
at me, a little shy, maybe, they look at me, at each other, and
what I think is that their faces look a little scared. I remain
standing in the hall.

Come in then, Knut says.

It's a long time since I was here, I say.

Ten, fifteen years, Knut says.

Aren't you coming in, Knut's wife calls from the living
room.

He's coming, Knut says, and he speaks into the living
room, to his wife, and once more I notice something foreign
in his voice, something that wasn't what it used to be, because
Knut told his wife that I, that I was coming, and I don't quite
understand what he means by that, and I remain standing in

the hall, and then the door to the kitchen begins to open and Knut's mother puts her head around the door, then the door opens fully and Knut's mother is standing there, broad, in the middle of the doorway, and she claps her hands together. She claps her hands together, and she smiles, and she says, well if it isn't, no it can't be, yes it is, she says, rocking on her feet as she stands there in the door to the kitchen, and she says that it's been a long time, what a long time it's been since she last saw me in this house, well, she says, it's such a long time ago that Knut was just a little boy when I was last here, she says. She'll have to come into the living room, too, Knut calls from the living room, his mother has to come into the living room as well. And his mother winks at me from the kitchen door, makes a grimace with her mouth, and then she says to me why don't I go into the living room. I start walking, I walk across the floor, I walk into the living room, I look around, and everything is as it has always been. Knut sits in a chair at the window, and he's leaning his elbows on the window ledge. Knut's hair is messy. He is looking out of the window. His wife sits on the sofa, in the middle of the sofa. In the living room at Knut's house everything is the way I remember it. The same pictures on the walls, the wedding photo of Knut's parents, the chest painted with the traditional pattern, the dining table, the big, heavy wooden sideboard, with all the intricate wood carvings, and they, the wood carvings, were made by Knut's grandfather, he actually made both the sideboard and the dining table, I remember that well, I can't remember who told me, but it was most probably Knut's mother, and the sofa, the one with the woven throw, the red and orange throw, then the armchairs, the radio, the big old radio. I hear Knut saying he's sure I remember this room, and I say yes I do, no changes here, I say, everything's exactly the way it used to be, and Knut says that's how she is, his mother, there's nothing to do about that, she'd rather keep everything the way it has always been, wouldn't hear of changing anything.

It's nice and comfy here, Knut's wife says.

She looks at me, and I don't know what to answer.

Why don't you sit down, Knut says.

I sit down in the armchair no one else is sitting in, it stands next to a round table, pretty much in the middle of the room. Along the left wall is the sofa, Knut's wife sits there, and Knut sits in front of me, on a chair at the window. Now that I'm sitting down I've got to say something, can't just sit there and say nothing, damn stupid of me to go for a walk along the main road, to allow her to drag me up here, it's all so long ago, it's so long ago since Knut and I used to be together, we don't have anything to say to each other, and Knut was dreading the thought of seeing me again, but he and his family had to go on holidays somewhere, and here, well it's cheap and easy to spend your holidays here in the village, it doesn't cost much, it's safe for the kids, the only thing is that he'll be forced to meet old friends, people he used to know, people he no longer has anything in common with, people he has distanced himself from, people it's better to think of as childhood memories, and that's how, that's exactly how, I feel as well. That's how it is. I have nothing to say. I just sit here.

Do you like it here, Knut says.

It's not too bad.

Don't you get bored?

I've always lived here, you know.

But you can still get bored? Knut's wife says.

Now and then.

Do you see anyone? Knut says.

Now and then, I say.

Who?

Well, I suppose it's mostly Torkjell, you know, the teacher, I play with him.

Yes, you told me, Knut says, and again, I don't understand it, perhaps I've told him, I can't remember if I have told him, perhaps yesterday, down on the road, when I met Knut and his family the first time, perhaps I told him then, I don't know, and then Knut's wife says that she'd like to come and listen to us, wasn't it next Saturday, that's tomorrow already, she says, and I nod, I don't understand why Knut has to say that I've already told him, and his wife saying she'd like to come and listen to us, would like to come to the dance, and Knut doesn't say anything, just turns away, and I sit in the armchair, and then there are shouts and laughter in the hall, and Knut leaps up, runs into the hall, it becomes quiet, and Knut comes back to the living room again, stands in the doorway, and he says that this time someone else has to try and put those kids to bed, and his wife says that when he's putting the kids to bed they stay wide awake, he's the only one who goes to sleep, and Knut says that now it's her turn to put the kids to bed, it was her turn tonight anyway, he says, and Knut's wife gets up, smiles at me, shrugs her shoulders resignedly, doesn't even look at Knut, goes out the door, turns and says have a nice time, won't we, she'll get the kids to bed, she supposes it's her job, isn't it, she'll get those kids to go to sleep, she says, and Knut gets up, walks across the floor, closes the door. Knut goes over to the sofa and sits down.

That's how it is, he says.

Well, it's a long time since we saw each other, I say.

The years fly.

It's incredible.

But you've got yourself a family.

You can see how it is.

Yes, I say, and there is silence, total silence for some time, no one says anything, and it becomes very quiet, the whole house is quiet, silent, we sit in silence, and I look out of the window, look down toward the main road, down toward the fjord, I get up, go over to the window, look down, look down toward the fjord, toward the cove at the innermost point of the fjord, where I live, just above that cove, in a white house, I look at the boats that are moored there, rowboats, wooden boats, runabouts, dinghies, there are outboard motors on the boats, I stand in front of the window, I look down at the cove, below Knut's house, on the other side of the road, where there's only one boat, the one Knut's wife used yesterday, it's the neighbor's boat, she must have borrowed the boat, I'm thinking. Knut sits on the sofa, he gets up, comes and stands next to me, looks out of the window.

It's nice here, Knut says.

We stand and look out of the window.

You often go fishing? Knut asks, and I hear something in his voice, something, I don't know what it is, I hear something in his voice, there's something in it, and I say that it happens, not all that often, but it happens that I go fishing, I like it out on the fjord, especially in summer, that's when I go fishing, that's the only time of the year that I go fishing, in summer, it isn't just the fishing as such, I don't quite know what it is, but I like it, I enjoy being out on the fjord, and Knut says that he never did, ever since he was small he never liked being out on the fjord, he doesn't know why, that's just how it is, and we stand there, stand in the living room of Knut's house, Knut's wife has gone to put their two kids to bed, two little girls, and Knut and I stand in the living room, stand in front of the window that faces the main road, the house is quiet, and Knut says that he has plenty of grog, there's no shortage of that, and Knut says why don't we have a little party, no reason we shouldn't. That'd be nice, I say, and Knut goes and gets a bottle of whiskey, ice cubes, water, a couple of kitchen glasses, and he pours the drinks, we sit down in front of the window, he sits on the chair that has always stood in front of the window in the living room, I take the armchair over to the window, between us on the floor is a jug of water and ice cubes, a bottle of whiskey, and we sit in silence, we look out of the window. We look down on the fjord. We drink whiskey. It's getting dark, and Knut puts on the light in the living room. I ask Knut if his wife has gone to bed, and he says that she probably hasn't, it just takes its time to put the kids to bed, they've got used to staying up late during the summer holidays. She'll be down soon, he says. Then Knut asks me how I am, and I say not too bad.

There's no woman in your life, he says.

No, not really, I say.

Well, it's time you get one.

I don't answer, I think I can notice something in his voice, I don't know what it is, but I notice something in his voice.

She likes to fish, too, the wife, he says.

Yes, I say.

You two should meet out on the fjord, then, he says.

You should go out on the fjord, too.

Don't care much about fishing.

But it can be nice out on the fjord anyway.

Have never liked it much.

And you don't like travelling either, I heard my wife say—

No, not much.

But you like fishing—

Well, yes.

Yes, I see.

Are you still playing, I ask.

Not much. I'm a music teacher, teach a few other subjects as well, but don't get to play very much myself.

I play less and less too.

Just traditional dance now.

Mostly, you can earn a bit of money on that.

You don't have a job?

I shake my head.

Have never had one either?

Not a permanent job, well, yes, but not for long. I've always left.

Why?

I don't know.

That's just the way it is.

You don't like to work?

No—

Not at all?

Not in a permanent job at least.

But what about education, I mean, you can't just keep hanging around here?

No—

Nothing?

I read a lot, but—

You read a lot?

I nod, and Knut pours me another whiskey and one for himself, and I hear steps on the stairs.

There she is, Knut says.

You've been married quite a few years? I ask.

And Knut answers that it's not all that long ago since they got married, they were living together at first, it was after the second child was born that they got married, and I noticed that Knut has become a bit restless, he empties his glass, pours himself another one, sees that my glass is almost full still, and his wife comes into the living room, says that well, here are the men, drinking whiskey, finally the kids are asleep, she says, it'd be nice with a glass of wine now, she says, no whiskey for her, but a glass of wine would be nice, and Knut says there's lots of wine in the house, and she says yes, she knows, and she's going to get a bottle of wine, she says, and Knut pours, fills up his glass, drinks.

Come on, drink up, he says.

I don't drink all that often, I say.

No, I don't suppose you've got a lot of people to drink with.

And the closest off-licence's some distance away.

You go into town often?

No, hardly ever.

You keep to yourself at home.

I nod, and Knut's wife comes back to the living room, she's carrying a bottle of wine and a kitchen glass, there aren't any proper glasses here, she says, just these kitchen glasses, but you can drink from them too, at least the wine's good, she says, and then she sits down on the sofa, her legs apart, puts the wine bottle on the floor, between her legs, screws the corkscrew into the cork, pulls, she pulls as hard as she can, and Knut and I sit and watch her, and Knut asks if she wants any help, and she says no, that's a new one, he isn't usually interested in helping, she's not interested in any help, she can manage, she says, and Knut says all right, fine by him, if she doesn't want any help, that's fine by him. I don't know what to say. I drink whiskey. I look at her, she sits on the sofa, legs apart, she has a wine bottle standing on the floor, and she is pulling the corkscrew. I get up, go over to her, take the corkscrew and the bottle, sit down on the sofa, put the bottle between my thighs and pull. I put the opened wine bottle on the sofa table and go back to the armchair by the window and sit down.

Well done, Knut says.

Did you see that, his wife says.

Yes, I did, Knut says.

I drink whiskey.

Why'd you do that? Knut asks.

No special reason, I say.

Because you like my missus, he says.

Yes, perhaps, I say.

Do you hear that, he likes you, likes my missus, Knut says, and turns to her.

Well, you certainly don't, she says.

I suppose you like him, too, Knut says, and he empties his glass, pours himself another, pours me one.

Of course I like him, she says.

I could see that yesterday already, he says.

Trying to seduce him, out there on the small island.

I thought so.

It's all you can think about, isn't it.

What?

That other men are fucking me.

Come on, stop it.

I'll stop it, she says, and she gets up, picks up her glass, takes a few steps, stops, says why don't we listen to some music, we're just talking rubbish, it's not going anywhere, it's the same night after night, she says, it isn't going anywhere, she says, and she stands in the middle of the floor, she holds her glass right in front of her, and Knut looks at her before he turns around again and looks out of the window, I, too, look out of the window, it is darker outside, but not dark, but the evenings are already becoming noticeably darker, and I should never have come up to the house, don't understand why she asked me to come, perhaps it was just to pester

Knut, because she knew that he was dreading the thought of meeting me and his other childhood friends again, that's why she asked me to come up here, I can't understand why else she wanted me to come, and Knut sits there, looking out of the window, and she stands on the floor, drinking wine, we sit and drink whiskey, and I must go, but it's difficult to get away, not so easy to say that you want to go, perhaps I should stay, I was only taking a walk along the road, and she, that's how it must have been, she saw me walking along the road, and so she came after me, to get me, to fetch me, and yesterday, out on the fjord, she saw me then too and did a turn around the cove below Knut's house, and she saw me steering the boat toward the small island, and she followed me, found me, and when I was unable to see anything but her eyes it was because she didn't want me to see anything else, perhaps she said that to Knut as well, said that your friend's out fishing, I want to have a chat with him, and then she went to the neighbor and borrowed their boat, asked if it was all right to use their boat, and she was Knut's wife, was on holiday here, for the first time, really, was here with their two daughters, that must be how it was, and I sit in the living room in Knut's house, his wife still stands on the floor, she has not put on any music, she has just talked about doing it, but hasn't done it, she just stands there, holding her wine glass, and Knut pours himself more whiskey, and I say I think I should be getting home, it's getting late, and Knut looks at me, says why don't I stay a bit longer, and she says that I mustn't go, then she and Knut will be alone, they are almost always alone, I mustn't go, she says, stay for a little

while, what's the rush, says Knut, it's not as if I have to go
to work tomorrow, of course I can stay, there's no rush at all,
we've got both women and wine, he says, and I want to get up,
leave, go home, everything's so long ago, there's nothing left,
everything's over, gone, must hurry, stand up, get on my feet,
must go home, and Knut pours himself more whiskey, mixes
it with water and ice, wants to pour me another, I move a flat
hand over the glass a couple of times, he puts the whiskey
bottle down on the floor again, and I stand up, empty my
glass, say I'd better be getting home, I stand there for a while,
and Knut's wife comes over to me and puts her arm around
my waist, leans into me, and she says that I mustn't go yet,
why don't I stay here with her, she says, I'm gorgeous, she
says, so cuddly, and then she laughs briefly, I just stand there,
she's holding me tight, I try to make her let go of me, she
keeps pressing the arm she has put around my waist against
my body, I feel her arm pressing against my skin, and she digs
her fingers into my side, strokes me with splayed fingers, and
then she puts the other arm around my stomach, smiles up
at me sideways, and I look into her dark eyes, her black hair,
and I feel her warmth against my body, and she leans into
me, I feel her warmth, and I look at Knut, he sits with his
back to us, looks out of the window, he has put his whiskey
glass on the windowsill, and she is quick to reach me with her
lips, kisses me wetly on the cheek, and Knut turns around, I
meet his eyes, and he shakes his head lightly. He says, that's
how she is, that's how his wife is. If only she had been drunk,
but she is completely sober, and she just stands there, in the
middle of the floor, right in front of him, and kisses and

hugs a man she has just met. He grins. Knut sits in his chair and grins. She lets go of me, sits down in the armchair, next to Knut, and I say well, I'd better be getting home. No one answers, and I walk into the hall, put on my jacket, my shoes. I can hear Knut saying why can't she ever learn, what is it she really wants, he says, what's she after, it's beyond him, and she repeats what he was saying, what's she after, can never learn, and I walk back in again, stand in the doorway, I stand there and tell them that I'll be going now, there's a dance on in the community hall tomorrow, so if they want to hear some proper traditional dance music why don't they come over. I walk out. I walked home, and the restlessness was strong. I had only just walked out the door when the restlessness came over me, and it was much stronger than the evening before, when I was inside the living room in Knut's house I didn't notice the restlessness, but it came over me when I was standing in the hall, and I knew I had to get home. I wanted to get away. Didn't want to show my face to anyone anymore. I wanted no one to see me again. I wanted to hide, to disappear. I was scared. I walked home at a fast pace, climbed the stairs to my attic, felt restless, scared, and I thought that something terrible would happen. That's why I'm restless, I thought, something inevitable is going to happen, something terrible. I walked home, and I was already starting to get nervous about Saturday night and playing with Torkjell. Traditional Dance in the Youth Hall. Featuring: Torkjell's Duo. I walked straight home, locked the door, made sure the door was properly locked. I went to bed, but I couldn't sleep, and my left arm started to ache, my fingers were aching. I was lying there for hours, the rest-lessness worrying me, I couldn't sleep, was just lying there in bed, tossing and turning, switching on the light, switching it off again, I tried to read, but I couldn't concentrate, I tossed and turned, I just kept lying there. It's a long time since the restlessness first came over me. I sit here and write, and I write because I want to keep the restlessness at bay, it helps to write. A restlessness has come over me. I don't know what it is, but this restlessness has come over me. This summer I met Knut again, I had not seen him for at least ten years, and then Knut just comes walking toward me. Knut and I were always together, played in a band together. My mother. I sit here and write, and below my mother is walking across the floor. The sound of her steps. The sound of her steps. My mother's not all that old. I have written quite a lot now, the pile of pages is mounting up. I don't go out anymore, don't play the guitar anymore. Must stop all this writing, my mother tells me. I don't listen to records anymore. I sit here and write. My left arm aches, my fingers ache. Knut's wife. Yellow rain jacket. Her denim jacket. Her eyes. I met Knut again this summer. Knut left. I don't go out anymore.

I sit here and write. I write for a reader. I don't go out anymore, and it's lonely here. I used to go to The Co-op to do the shopping, but now I don't go out anymore. I also did small jobs earlier, collected fruit, worked a little at The Co-op, tidied the storeroom and things like that. Besides there were quite a few playing jobs. Now I don't go out anymore. I don't want to play with Torkjell anymore. We haven't played together since the dance at the Youth Hall this summer. Knut and I. Knut's wife. I met Knut this summer, and it was then the restlessness came over me. I sit here and write. My mother is walking across the floor downstairs. This won't do, she says, my mother. She is not all that old. Knut's wife. A yellow rain jacket. Denim jacket. Her eyes. My mother is walking across the floor down there, and I can hear the sound of the television up here. Knut and I were always together. I don't know. I see Knut with a class friend. The pile of sheets has grown big now. I sit here and write. The writing removes the restlessness. I like to write, it makes me happy. My mother is walking around the house. I sit and write. I really don't have a bad life. I live here with my mother. I have never lived anywhere else. I hear my mother walking across the floor downstairs. The sound of the television. My mother is not all that old, she strokes my hair. This summer I met

Knut again. It was then the restlessness came over me, for
nothing is the way it once was, everything has changed.
Knut and I were always together. Now Knut is married, has
two daughters. Knut and I were children together, became
youths together. I saw Knut walking down the road, I called
after him. He didn't answer, just kept going. I met Knut
again this summer, he and his wife were at the dance at the
Youth Hall. Knut danced with an old class friend. Knut and
I, we were always together, went to the Children's Club in
the Youth Hall, and when the Children's Club finished,
when we'd finished with the hot buns and the hot chocolate,
with the songs and the folksong playing, when we were left
to ourselves, when we got to enter into it, when we had been
at the Children's Club in the Youth Hall, when we, when
Knut and I and the others had finished with what we had to
do, if we wanted to be in the Children's Club, then we could
run out of the large hall, out into the hallway, when there
were no more songs to be danced, when we ran out into the
hallway, lay down on the floor, when the others came running,
when the girls came, when that girl came. When she came.
When she came. When she came from all the lunch breaks,
from all the breaks you'd seen her in, when she came with
her long hair, with her small breasts which you saw there
behind her blouse, when she came running out into the
hallway, and you knew that you'd never dare to speak to her,
that you, who had made such noise and clamor there on the
floor, with Knut or one of my other friends, when she came
you became quiet, you stopped kicking your legs, stopped
fooling around, talking nonsense, talking in a loud voice, you

became quiet, became a little shy, you stood up from the floor, and suddenly you didn't know what to do with yourself, your heart became restless, because now she was there, she was close to you, with her hair, her body, she was just a few meters from you, so close to you, and you couldn't talk to her, even if she had sent you a message two days ago, one of her girlfriends had come giggling and said that she was coming to say hello to you from her, from her, from her with the long hair. When she stood there, calmly, stood there and talked with one of the other girls, there in the half-dim canteen in the Youth Hall, stood in the middle of the other children who attended the Children's Club, and everyone did that, almost all the children in the village went here, when she stood there, with her young breasts, with her long hair, and when she smiled to her girlfriend, and you stood there, stood there alone while the others made noises, then you felt a grief that grew large inside you. It was then it started. Something happened then. Perhaps it was then the music came to you. There and then, and since then you haven't managed to get away. And afterwards, after the Children's Club in the Youth Hall was finished, and you were going home. Everyone was going to their own place, but no one did. Then we walked along the road. Then a group of boys and girls walked along the road, away from where some of us lived and in the direction of where others lived. It was autumn, it was dark, and we walked along a narrow country road, in the rain, in the wind. We walked along the road, it was dark, and we heard the fjord. The sea which was there all the time. The waves. We walked along the road, there was me, there was Knut, there were several others, and she was there. She and Knut were talking together. I was talking to another girl, quite another girl, a totally different girl, a girl from my class, and we knew each other, could talk easily together, but I could never forget the other one, where she walked, a couple of meters ahead of me, with her hair, with her young breasts, behind her jacket, where she walked and talked with Knut. I walked with another girl, and perhaps that was the girl Knut wanted to walk with. We were talking and fooling around. She was walking ahead of me, and Knut put his arm around her back, she put her arm around Knut. I was walking behind Knut and her, with a girl from my class, and I put my arm around her shoulder, and she leaned lightly against me. We were talking and fooling around. A group of us were walking along the road, we were all in one of the final classes in primary school, some had just started comprehensive school. It was autumn, dark. Rain. We could hear the fjord. The waves. We walked along the road. We stopped on the road, above the boathouse, and Knut says that we can go in there, no one would notice, and Knut goes in first, we follow him, we go into the boathouse, in through the hatch on the side, and I climb up the ladder, up into the attic to get the candles, and then someone says something, one of those who always dares to, says that we can play kiss-pat-and-hug, no one answers, and everyone wants to, and then one of us takes the lead, lines us up, the first to go out stands in a corner, we others stand in a half-circle around, and the candles stand on the earthen floor in the boathouse, the brave one who thought of the game will get it started, the appointed one must say what he wants, kiss, pat, or hug, and then you do eenie meenie miney moe around the half-circle, until the one who is to kiss or clap is pointed out, first it's only clap, careful strokes over the cheeks, random boys and random girls stroke each other's cheeks, in an old boathouse, protected from the rain, it's an early autumn evening, and we can hear the fjord. The waves. Someone dares to say hug, and then he or she stands there, a little shy, a little brave and hug one of the other sex, clasping him or her tightly. Hugs quite briefly, hugs a little longer. The others are not staring, look away, look down, just glance at the two who stand there and hug each other. Time passes, we get used to the game, become safer, braver. The rain increases, the wind becomes stronger, and the waves that roll against the shore become more pro-nounced. The evening becomes blacker. We dare to move closer to each other. We say kiss, and when he who said it has got the girl assigned who is to be kissed, and when the one who is to kiss has moved out from the darkness, moving toward the one who is to be kissed, then no one looks in the direction of those two, then we look down. Then it's only the darkness and the rain that are around the two, the rest of us disappear into a silent loneliness, each of our own, and around the loneliness there's a calm collaboration, yes, a collaboration where no one says anything, but where we are close to each other, without being persons to each other, but we are there, and then it was her turn, and I notice her eyes in the darkness, catch a glimpse of her long hair, she has said kiss, and I wish with all of me that it isn't me she is going to kiss, it must be Knut, because it's Knut she wants to kiss, not me, it mustn't be me, I think with all of me, and then it turns out to be me, and I have to move out of the dark community, with my hair, with my body, and she moves toward me, I stand there, don't hear the rain, only notice how I have pushed forward, all I want is to come back to the wordless others, as I stand there in my wet jacket, my hands straight down, and she's moving quickly toward me, coming out of the darkness, with her eyes, with her hair, and she puts both her arms around me, we stand there jacket against jacket, my hair is wet, and I feel her hand stroking my back, and then she moves her half-open mouth against my cheek, the warmth from her lips, her mouth, the moisture, a warm moisture, that's all, there in the boathouse the darkness, the rain, and then we had to keep walking, we climbed out through the side hatch in the boathouse, the whole group, one after the other, and then we kept walking on the black road, along the shore, some places the waves were rolling almost up to the road, we kept walking, I was walking behind the others, ahead of me were Knut and her, they held around each other's shoulders, we walked as far as The Co-op, there we stopped, stood there, stood there in the light of the shop windows, I stood with a girl from my class, we talked and fooled around, we talked together the way we always did, I tried to be the way I'd always been, and when we walked toward home I took her hand, and we held hands along the road, until we arrived at her place, then we hugged each other and she went inside, and I walked along with the others, we walked homewards, heard the waves, both she and Knut were still with us, they walked and held each other's hands, they were both silent, we were all silent, and I had come home to my house, said bye, ran up to my place, up the road, told my mother I wasn't hungry, walked up to my room. That was really how it started. It was evenings like that, after we had been to Children's Club in the Youth Hall, had been to something or other, it was such dark autumn evenings after the adults had finished their parental duties, and we were by ourselves, alone, were there together, with all the things we had to do, it was evenings like that, when we were walking along the roads, boys and girls, when we were there by ourselves, with our own things, that it started, it started with her, she with the long hair, she who Knut used to walk hand in hand with, she with the young breasts, she was there for a long time, several years, and still, here I sit alone, sit here and write, and downstairs I can hear the sound of my mother's television, this is a house in which you can hear every sound, an old white house, and I can still feel her moist lips against my cheek, there in the rain, in the dark, I can hear how the waves were rolling in, and I notice it as something that has fastened itself to my body, to my movements. This is how it started, in the darkness, in the rain, on a road lying along the foreshore, in an old boathouse, it was the waves that were always rolling in, and the skin that grew bigger and bigger. Her kiss was a mark on my skin, that pushed itself into my body and remained there. She was married now, had big kids, is a housewife, and she and her husband used to go to the community dances. They were there this summer, when we played. Torkjell and I. He played accordion, I played guitar. She was at the community dance, but now her body has changed. She was dancing with Knut.

Her hair is short. Her breasts had become much bigger. Everything is different. I met Knut again this summer, I hadn't seen him for at least ten years. I sit here and write, my mother is walking across the floor downstairs, I keep hearing her walking on the floor. I hear the sound of the television. I don't know. I write to keep the restlessness at bay, but it only becomes bigger. I'm calm when I write, but then, right afterward, the restlessness comes back, something is going to happen, something terrible, I know it. I don't go out anymore, I stay inside. A restlessness has come over me. My mother is walking across the floor downstairs. I hear her steps, the sound of the television. I don't go out anymore.

I met Knut again this summer, and it was then the restlessness came over me. My mother. Knut's wife. A yellow rain jacket. Denim jacket. Her eyes. I hadn't seen Knut for at least ten years. The evening after I met Knut again we played at the community dance. Torkjell's Duo. Knut danced with an old class friend. I can't count the times I played to a dance in the Youth Hall. A restlessness has come over me. I have finished playing, I tell Torkjell that I don't want to play anymore. I don't go out anymore. I met Knut again this summer. A restlessness has come over me. Knut and I. It was there we rehearsed, in the Youth Hall. Torkjell and I never rehearse anymore, I refuse, tell him I don't want to rehearse, I haven't done any more playing jobs either. I don't go out anymore. I sit here and write, that's all. But we hardly rehearsed before either, and if we had to rehearse, we rehearsed at Torkjell's. Now I don't go out anymore. We played this summer at the community dance, and since then I haven't wanted to play with Torkjell any longer. I don't go out anymore. My mother is walking across the floor down there in the living room. I hear the sound of the television up here. A restlessness has come over me, my left arm aches, my fingers. My mother is not so old. It was two days after I met Knut again that we played at the community dance. As usual, there were only a few people there when we began to play, the odd couple. Torkjell stands at the front, a meter behind the edge of the stage, a small amplifier behind him, and I stand to the left of Torkjell, well behind him, and behind me stands a small amplifier. Waltz, the couple dance. I strum the guitar, chord after chord. I look at the hall, it's almost empty, no one's dancing, I look at Torkjell. He stands the way he always stands, his left foot far forward, his head a little tilted, and his torso swaying back and forth to the rhythm of the tune he's playing. Now and then he tosses his head. Now and then he smiles. I stand straight up and down. We play through the first set of songs. There are still only a few people in the hall when we take the first break. I sit down in the coulisses on the stage, there are chairs stacked there, many stacks, I sit high up, on one of the stacks, there are a lot of empty bottles on the floor. I hear people talk down there in the hall. I just sit there. Then Torkjell comes jumping over the edge of the stage, and he says that we've got to start working again. There'll soon be quite a few people here, he says. We get ready. Get going with a waltz. Suddenly the floor is full. Someone sings here and there. I look at Torkjell, he has truly livened up. He's enjoying himself now. He smiles almost all the time. Tosses his head. His fringe falls onto his forehead, he tosses it up again, the same again. People are dancing. We are playing. The hall is getting fuller and fuller. In the breaks between two numbers the talking in the hall becomes loud. People are dancing. Now and then someone claps when we've finished a tune. I stand straight up and down, strum the chords. I know most of those who are dancing. Married couples, most

of them, some of them bachelors. A few old girls. Almost
no young people. I strum and strum the chords. There I see
Knut, he and his wife are standing down by the door. I nod
to them. We play. I see Knut swinging across the floor, he's
dancing with one of the older women, one he went to school
with. His wife is standing there by the door. Knut is dancing
with a girl he went to school with for nine years, in the same
class. I see her husband going over to Knut's wife, bowing,
asking her to dance, but she shakes her head, she smiles, she
says something to the man, he turns quickly, turns his back
to her, and he lifts his foot, his foot at an angle, and then he
smacks his shoe with the flat of his hand, and once more
he stands and faces her, he smiles, she says something, and
he says something. We play. Number after number, I strum
the chords. Knut dances. And his wife stands down by the
door, talking to a man, I don't know him, have never spoken
to him, the man is a good deal older than his wife, the one
who's dancing with Knut, and then I see Knut's wife and
the man go over to the wall running lengthwise, on my side,
they walk forward, almost all the way to the stage, and they
sit down, there are benches along the wall, wooden benches,
and there are vacant places close to the stage, on the bench
which is on my side, and they sit down there. They talk.
Knut's wife looks at me, smiles to me. I smile back. The man
talks. After a while he gets up and walks a little further along
the bench, asks a girl who sits there to dance. He starts to
dance. Knut's wife sits on the bench, up at the front. She
sits alone. She looks at me. Black hair, her eyes. Thick and
short hair. Her eyes. Denim jacket. Knut dances, and then

I can't see him anymore. His wife sits on the bench. A few
young people have arrived now. A group of boys have walked
toward the stage, over in the left corner, I can't see them, but
they stand in the corner next to the stage, on the left side, in
front of where Knut's wife is sitting. A couple of them are
already pretty tipsy. Torkjell finishes a tune, pulls a long note,
nods to me, then he pulls in his protruding foot, it stands stiff
and aslant while he plays, then he twists off one of the straps
on the accordion, pushes the accordion together, fastens the
clamps, puts it away, on the edge of the stage. I remove my
guitar. Turn off the amplifier. Put the guitar at an edge along
the amplifier. I walk into the hall, notice that ten or so youths
have gathered in the corner, around the tiled stove that stands
there, it's summer now, no need to heat the stove. They are
standing in a group. They stand and drink. A couple of older
people walk over to them, too. Knut's wife sits on the bench
next to them. There's a break now, and many are on their way
out. To get a bit of fresh air and a swig. I can't be bothered
going out, walk up toward the stage again, walk up the stairs
to the stage, I don't look around. Then someone's calling,
and Knut's wife is on her way toward me. I see the gang over
in the corner turning around and looking at her. I stop, she
asks if I want to have a chat, and I walk down into the hall
again, she walks over to the bench along the wall, sits down.
I walk over to her. I notice a couple of young boys turning
around, they grin at me. I sit down. She puts her hand on
my upper arm, turns to me. More people from the gang over
by the stove turn to us. They're pretty pissed, I see. Knut's
wife holds her hand on my upper arm, turns to me. A few

more people from the gang around the stove turn to us. I can
see they're pretty drunk. Knut's wife holds her hand on my
upper arm. I ask her if she's enjoying herself, and she says
it's interesting, she has never been to a community dance,
not like this kind of dance, has been to ordinary community
dances, many times, but that's different, she has never been
to anything like this, it's really quite an experience. She talks
quickly. I don't know what to say. I couldn't have imagined
it'd be like this, she says, but she can't see Knut, she says, and
there's no one she knows here, he'll probably come soon,
Knut, she says, and have I seen him. I say that I haven't seen
him for a while, I saw him dancing, since then I haven't seen
him, and she says that she is not very good at dancing traditional dance, has never learned it, and then she'll just have
to sit here till he turns up, she says. He'll probably come
soon, perhaps he has met some old friends, I say. But it's so
boring to sit here alone, she says. She holds her arm lightly
on my upper arm. He'll come soon, I say. One of the young
boys in the group breaks loose, staggers a little more than he
should, turns, walks onto the floor, turns again, looks at the
wall where we sit, looks down at us. He fixes his eyes on me.
He squints at me.

So you've found a woman, now, he says.

I look at him.

Time you did, damn it.

No, I say in a drawl.

I can see you've found a woman, he says.

Not my woman, I say.

You sit there and smooch, he says and he staggers over

to the gang again, stands there, a little outside of the group now, pulls at the jacket sleeve on one of them who is just standing there, gets him a little out on the floor.

Look, he says and looks at us, and the guy looks obediently at us with a worried expression on his face.

Look who's sitting there, he says. Don't you see, hah! He's found a woman now.

The other fellow glances quickly at me.

She's a looker too, isn't she, he says. Damn it, what a great woman. Certainly about time you found a woman, can't fuck with the guitar, damn it.

I toss my head.

Damn great woman, too, he says. Fuck it, it should be—

He prods his friend, and they begin to laugh. They tumble together along the dance floor, toward the exit. I notice that her hand pinches my upper arm hard. One of the young guys, the one who came first, I know who he is, but I've never spoken to him, I've seen his friend, too, but I don't know who he is either, both of them are often at the dances, and both come back, his friend goes over to the group that stands around the stove, he stands up on the floor, right in front of us, and I feel her hand squeezing my upper arm harder, and she whispers in my ear that we should go somewhere else, this is too childish, she says, and I nod.

Damn it, look at them necking, the boy says.

I stand up.

Are you going to fuck now, he says, and he makes a circle with his thumb and forefinger on his left hand, puts his forefinger on his right hand through, holds his hands in front of him.

Damn it all, he's going to fuck, he says.

We begin to walk across the floor.

Wish it was me who's going to fuck, the fellow says.

I look behind me, he has turned after us.

My god, the fiddler-fucker has found a woman, he says, and he almost roars now. Poor damn woman, he says.

Loud guffaws are heard from the corner, I look over there, and the whole gang stands there looking at the guy. Their eyes follow us. Grin. We walk up on the stage.

He's going to fuck her behind the stage, yells the kid, and he waves his hands, before he walks backward, turns, walks toward the exit door, and we walk behind the edge of the stage. I sit down on the pile of chairs. There are chairs for her too, I say, but she only shakes her head, sits down on my lap, and she puts her arm around my neck. She puts her arm around my neck. Suddenly I feel her lips against my cheek. They are moist. I feel her mouth move down to my ear, she licks my earlobe lightly, light shivers run through my body, and she whispers that she wants to sit here behind the stage somewhere, she wants to sit there till the dance is over, and then she wants the two of us to walk home together, she whispers, licks my earlobe, and I nod, then she squeezes her lips against my cheek, spread lips, moist, and then her tongue, lightly over my skin, and I just sit there and she whispers that it's only what he deserves, it's all nonsense anyway, she'd rather be with me, she says, and she whispers in a low voice, and then she laughs briefly, squeezes my shoulder, presses her nose against my cheek, and I put my arm around her shoulders, she puts her head against my chest. I hold her tightly. I hear her laughing quietly against my chest, and then I notice that she puts a hand on my stomach, in through the opening between the buttons on my shirt, and her fingers play lightly with the hairs on my stomach. We sit behind the stage, we can hear from the buzz of voices that people have started to enter the hall again. I hold my arm around her shoulders, and I pull my arm back, and she pulls her hand back, and she's still sitting on my lap, and she holds her arm around my shoulder. I only look straight ahead.

Have you finished now?

It roars from the hall, the kid's voice, and I hear someone come stamping up the stage stairs.

Have you finished fucking now?

I see him standing over by Torkjell's amplifier, staggering even more now, much more than necessary, and I see he's hiding a bottle in his right hand, behind the sleeve of his jacket. He moves toward us.

Was she a good fuck? he says and stares at me.

Take it easy now, I say.

Looks good, he says, and I feel her hand squeeze my shoulder hard and quickly.

So you didn't sit there and smooch, he says, moves closer, stands next to me, looks around, and then he pulls out a pocket flask, takes a swig, hands me the bottle, I shake my head.

What the fuck, he says.

Don't drink when I'm playing, I say.

Idiot, he says. Of course the musician must have a drink.

It becomes more than one then, I say.

What the fuck, he says.

You'd better get down in the hall again, I say.

I like your woman so much, he says

I toss my head, he takes another swig, grimaces, hands me the bottle, and lifts his hands up deprecatingly.

All right then, he says.

Go now, I say.

Was she a good fuck? he asks.

Stop now, I say.

What the fuck, he says.

Just calm down, I say.

What a fucking fine woman, he says, and I breathe out resignedly, he stands there holding his bottle, puts the bottle down on the floor, bends his neck forward, looks in his pockets with both hands, finds a packet of tobacco, pulls it out, rolls a cigarette painstakingly, thin in one end, thick in the other, so thick that the cigarette paper becomes too narrow, the tobacco sticks out of the thick end, he tries to light the cigarette with a match, doesn't manage to do it, tears off the thinnest end, tries to light it again, and now he succeeds, and so he bends down again, picks up the bottle of spirits, pulls up the cork, drinks, and I see Torkjell come walking up the stairs to the stage, moves with the same quick movements he always uses, ready for a new session, he looks over at us, sees the young boy's back, he turns around, and Torkjell roars, what the hell's he doing up here, and the guy's about to say something, but Torkjell has already joined him, the guy has tried to put the bottle behind his jacket, and Torkjell grins, says what the fuck does he have there, he's got to show him what he has, the guy just stands there, staggers a little, keeps his hand in his jacket, and then Torkjell pulls his hand out from the jacket, just what I thought, he says. Torkjell says that the guy has to get down from the stage, and in a damn hurry too. The guy just stands there. All right then, Torkjell says, twists the bottle of spirits out of the boy's hand. Takes his arm and leads him toward the edge of the stage. The guy resists. Torkjell's grip becomes harder. The guy resists. Torkjell swears, damn you, he says, Satan, he twists the boy's arm, twists hard, the boy stands there, resists, keeps resisting, they're at a standstill, before we can see that Torkjell twists so hard that the boy's back bends forward, bends even more, and then Torkjell pushes him and he falls forward over the edge of the stage, hits the floor. I'm standing now. I stand a little behind Torkjell. The guy stays on the floor. People are gathering around him, a few from the gang of boys have moved toward him. They stand and look at the boy lying on the floor. After a while he struggles to stand up. There's blood on his forehead. He walks toward the exit. Torkjell looks at me. He says that damn it, you can't treat things like that with a light hand. He's had enough trouble with that devil. Was his teacher for too many years. He should've given him a proper belting, once and for all. That woman, he says. Is she going to sit there? I nod, say that she would like to sit there while we play, and Torkjell says that if that's what she wants, he's got nothing against it. But we'd better get started again. Torkjell lifts up his accordion, I pick up my guitar, turn on the amplifier. We've got to have a little bit of mood. Then we're at it again. I notice in Torkjell's movements that he's had a drink or two on the break. He plays better now. The hall is full. They smoke and dance. I stand there, straight up and down, and strum the chords. I know that she sits there looking at me, but I don't want to turn around. Knut's wife. I play. People dance. I see Knut dancing. He's dancing with a girl he used to go to school with. Knut dances. We play, number after number. I don't turn around. It's the last dance, and Torkjell shouts it. The last dance, he calls. Now everyone must get on the floor. He waits a little. I see Knut struggling his way across the hall, he's coming up to the edge of the stage, waves to me, asks if I have seen his wife. I hear him through the buzz of voices. I shake my head. He says that he hasn't seen her for a while, she's probably gone home, he'll take a round through the hall, and Torkjell's already playing the last waltz. I'm late, I wait till the right moment, then I join him on the guitar, and it sounds good. I watch Knut walking around the hall, along the benches, until I can't see him anymore. The last dance, and we've finished. A little sparse applause. I turn, walk behind the stage, still with the guitar hanging around my neck. She's still sitting there. I tell her that Knut was looking for her, asking after her, just now, just before we started playing the last dance, she says that as far as she's concerned, he can just keep looking, she isn't interested in seeing him, he's sure to have gone home, she told him that she didn't like it here, wanted to go home, she says, and she's sure he believes that she's gone home, she says, and I nod, take my guitar off, find the guitar case, unplug the guitar, pack it up, find the cover to the amplifier, cover it, and I can't see Torkjell, but his accordion is still there, his amplifier's lit up, I take his equipment as well, put it all in a corner. The hall is almost empty now. The floor is gray. Empty bottles are lying along the walls, the air is full of smoke. Someone has started to tidy up. I don't know what to do, I notice that she's looking at me. Don't quite know. I say it's time to get home, and she gets up. I walk down into the hall, walk out, several groups are gathered outside the Youth Hall, I begin to walk slowly along the road. I notice that she is coming after me. I stop. She catches up. We walk next to each other along the road. There's still a long row of cars alongside the road, people haven't gone home yet from the dance. They loiter, dawdle. A few cars pass us. We walk slowly. We walk past the row of cars. We walk along the roadside. We don't say anything. Cars are passing us. Car after car. I turn around, and now there are only a couple of cars outside the Youth Hall. We walk. She walks next to me, and I don't know what to say to her. Knut's wife. She can't find Knut, and I don't know what to say, we walk next to each other, she walks closest to the road, I walk right at the edge, the evening is at its darkest, it's a summer evening, but still almost totally dark, and I don't know what to say, but I notice something strange, I don't know what to say, but it doesn't really matter, we're walking next to each other, we don't say anything, just walk, and then, suddenly, she puts her hand under my arm, we walk and her body comes closer and closer to my body, and her fingers clasp and stroke the pit of my elbow. We walk along the road, it's almost totally dark, all the houses are dark. We catch a glimpse of cars in the yards, they twinkle through the darkness. We don't talk. Her fingers play in the pit of my elbow, and I hear a car coming behind us, and I let go of her. She laughs lightly at me. The car passes us, and once more she puts her hand under my arm.

You're afraid they'll see us, she says.

I nod.

You don't talk much, she says.

Does that scare you, I say.

I notice that she nods, I don't look at her, look the other way, but I notice that she nods, nods quite lightly, and she is close to me, and it doesn't matter, it doesn't frighten me, it doesn't matter that I don't know what to say either, that's what it should be like, and her hand, her finger, her body, she is close to my body again, very close, and we walk there, along the road, along the fjord, and the waves are rolling in slowly, again and again, rolling against the shore, and the fjord is black, stretching outward, and I catch a glimpse of the mountains along the fjord, dark houses, and the fjord, again and again the fjord and the waves, and then the mountains. I say that she'll soon be home now, and she says that she doesn't want to go home, would rather be with me, and I shudder, and then I notice the restlessness again, the same restlessness that came over me the evening before, and she notices that something isn't as it should be, asks if everything's alright, she can easily go home if that's the way it is, she says, and we keep going, now something has to happen, I notice, she doesn't want to go home, she says she wants to be with me, and Knut has disappeared, doesn't want to go home, be with me, something must happen, find something, be with me, and we can't go home to my place, my mother, she has to go back to her place, and we catch a glimpse of the house of Knut and his family, we walk a little more slowly, she holds my arm, and Knut can see it, he was nowhere to be seen in the Youth Hall, he must have gone home, he was nowhere, he asked me about his wife, if I'd seen her, and I said I hadn't, I hadn't seen her, why did I say that, she was sitting behind the stage, I should've said where she was, I couldn't do that, and we approach Knut's house, and she whispers that she doesn't want to go home, she wants to be with me, she says, only wants to be with me, doesn't want to go home, and I say that we can't go home to my place, that's not possible, I say, and she says all right, and the pressure in the pit of my elbow lightens, and we have arrived at the road leading up to Knut's house, and she says that she wants at least to walk a little bit further with me, walk along the road with me, surely she can do that, she says, and I nod, keep walking slowly. Now the restlessness is very distinct. The restlessness moves through my whole body. A distinct restlessness. We walk slowly. I must say something. I don't notice the fjord any longer, now that she is so calmly close to me. A restlessness in my body. We walk. Something must happen. Cannot go home to my place. She holds my arm, and Knut can see us. He went home from the dance. We walk along the road, we have walked past Knut's house, and she says that she doesn't want to go home, wants to be with me. She says that she wants to be with me. Can't go home to my place. And Knut can see us. See that she's holding my arm. We walk along the road. The darkness, and the fjord. Must say something. Can't just walk here. We walk along the fjord. The waves. Always these waves. Say something. We walk past the boathouse, it's old, in disrepair. I tell her that in this boathouse Knut and I often played when we were little kids, no one uses the boathouse, there's a half-rotten rowboat in there, a few other things, old fishing gear, old cotton seines which are so brittle that they fall apart if you touch them, old fishing nets, the boathouse has an earthen floor, I say, but up on the attic, and there's a ladder up to it, we were often up there, we made a kind of den there, with candles and all sorts of things, we had lots of fun there, I say. She says that we formed a kind of boys' club then. I say that's exactly what we did. A secret club. It was only Knut and me who knew about the club. She stops and her hand tightens around mine.

Let's go up there, she says.

I hesitate.

Oh come on, she says.

But it's dark and very dusty in there, I say.

That doesn't matter.

I remain standing on the road, and I think that I shouldn't have said what I did about the boathouse, shouldn't have done it, why did I have to say it, just a silly thing to say. Can't go into the boathouse. Knut's wife, cannot do it.

Don't dawdle, she says.

I just stand there, and she takes my hand, folds our hands together, asks if my name wasn't Lcif, and then she leads me down the quarry, asks me where the door to the boathouse is, and I say there are two doors, a big one on the lower side, to pull the boats in and out through, a double door, and then a small door on the other side, almost a hatch, that was the one Knut and I used, I say, and she says that we'll have to use that one, then, and I nod, say that's the only thing we can do, the big door can only be opened from inside, I say, there's a beam across it, which has to be removed to open the door. She laughs. I say it's dark in there. She says that she has a lighter. And I'd said there were candles in there, she says. We hold each other's hands. We go behind the boathouse, we struggle to make our way between a few branches, I find the door, and suddenly I feel her lips against my cheek, and at the same moment the restlessness comes over me, and then I feel her lips fumble their way toward my mouth, she presses her lips against my mouth, and I hear the waves rolling, I notice the restlessness, she stands in front of me, holds both hands around my back, holds them folded behind my back, and her tongue pushes its way in between my lips, touches my tongue, and there's a restlessness in me. We stand there. I hear the waves rolling against the shore. The waves. We just stand there, and then she says that perhaps we should get inside the boathouse. She wants to see what it's like in there, she says. I open the small door, bend down, crawl in, she follows, it's totally dark in here, she lights a lighter, and I look around in the weak shimmer of light, it's many years since I've been here, perhaps more than twenty years, I think, and everything seems to be exactly how it was, the same smell, and I just stand there, she comes over to me, flings her arms and body around me, lets her tongue play over my cheeks, and I don't think about anything, say suddenly, must just say something, why don't we climb up to the attic, and she nods, so we go over to the ladder, and we climb up the ladder, she first, then I. We stand up there, on the wooden floor, and once more she lights her lighter. I look around. Everything is the way it was. Plastic bottles and empty bottles spread around. The things Knut and I have found on the shore. I stand there. Knut's wife has sat down on a bench we made, from an old seine, we filled the seine with a few old flour sacks. She sits down. She sits down on the bench Knut and I made. I keep standing. She says that I must come over to her. Not exactly warm here. Pretty raw air, she says. I just stand there. She says that I must come over to her. Come on now, she says. I go over and sit down next to her, and she puts her arm around my waist, leans against me, but I just sit there, she kisses my neck, smiles at me, and the restlessness aches in me, I don't know what to do, what to do with myself, must say something, the restlessness is great, must say something, do something, I've gone home from the dance, don't know where Knut is, and his wife, she holds her arms around me, and I don't know what to do, must say something, the restlessness is great, must say something, and I say that I'll have to start getting home. She says that surely we can stay there for a while. It's time to go home, I say. She asks if I'm tired, and I say yes I'm tired, it's demanding to play for a whole evening, I say, and she nods. I stand up, and then I hear the waves, I hear the waves, I hear something I had forgotten, I suddenly hear it. I hear the waves, the fjord, and the restlessness is very obvious in my body. I remain standing, and Knut's wife asks if everything's all right, if something special has happened, why do I stand there like that, I look very strange, she says, and I don't have to go home already, she says, why can't we stay here a little longer, and I stand there, just stand there, and she says that if I'm just going to stand there and look quite mad, we may as well leave, she says, and I nod. She stands up. I hear the waves, I hear the waves the way I heard them a long time ago, and I stand there, and I look at her, she blows out the candle, and it becomes totally dark. She puts out the lighter. She says that I must go first, and with a great restlessness in my body, and with an utterly black darkness around me I climb down the ladder step by step, and all the time I hear the waves, and the restlessness is great, my left arm aches, my fingers, I hear the waves, the way I used to hear them before, when I was a boy, when Knut and I played together, had our secret life, in the boathouse, in the attic there, and I climb down the ladder, step by step, slowly, and it's dark around me, I hear the waves, and I notice the movements from the waves in my body, step by step down the ladder, and I stand on the earthen floor, feel the smell of earth, hear the waves, and it's dark, totally dark. I see nothing, but then I hear a lighter being lit, turn, see the flame from the lighter, and at the outskirt of the flame is Knut's wife, her black hair, her brown eyes, and the restlessness in my body is great. I'm standing down in the boathouse. Knut's wife has lit a lighter. I hear the waves, and the restlessness is great. I must say something.

I'd better get home now, I say.

Yes, I understand that, she says.

I just stand there.

Well, we'd better go then, she says.

I walk out first, wait outside until she has come out, and then I close the hatch, but I don't put on the hook, just shove the hatch shut, Knut's wife is waiting, I stop, suddenly, remain standing there, she stands there too, quite still, and she is close to me, I stand still, don't know what to do, what to say, I just stand there, must do something, and then I begin to walk, struggle through the branches and the bushes, and all the time I notice the restlessness, I hear the waves, they don't roll in the way they used to, but in a different way, the way they used to do earlier, a long time ago, it's just that now I hear them through a restlessness, I walk, struggle through the scrub, hear Knut's wife walking behind me, she walks so close to me, I notice her close to my body. I must say something, do something. I walk up toward the main road, I don't turn around, don't say anything, but I notice that Knut's wife is coming, and I am restless, my left arm aches, my fingers. I walk slowly, stop, and she walks past me, I notice her hand stroking my back, I stand quietly, she has passed me, and then I begin to walk slowly uphill, behind her, and she stops at the roadside, stands there in the darkness, and I climb up the road, stand a few meters away from her, and I say I'd better get home, and she says yes, I've already said that, I say bye, she looks at me, turns, begins to walk the other way, she walks out along the road, toward Knut's house, I walk the other way, walk inland, and I hear the waves, I think that she didn't say bye to me, and the restlessness in my body is great, a heavy restlessness, and I hurry, try to walk with long steps, I can't begin to run, I think, and I walk along the road, hear the waves, I hear the waves the way I heard them when I was a boy, they roll and roll, throughout my whole life they have rolled, again and again, they roll and roll, and I haven't heard them for many years, not since I was a boy have I heard the waves, and now I hear them through a great restlessness. I hurry homeward. I hear the waves. I walk. I walk homeward as fast as I can. The waves are rolling against the shore. I walk homeward, and I can't concentrate my thoughts about anything, everything is inside a great restlessness, and in the movements of the waves. Knut's wife. I walk homeward, hurry, I must get home, and the restlessness is great, I hear and hear the waves. I sit here and write, and I don't go out anymore. It was this summer that I met Knut again. It was then that the restlessness came over me. I don't know. My mother. I don't play the guitar anymore. I don't know what it is. A restlessness has come over me, my left arm aches, my fingers. I haven't been to the library since early summer. My mother walks across the floor, and I can hear the sound of the television up here. I sit here and write, day after day I sit here and write, I never go out, my mother does the shopping, I would often do the shopping, now I say no, I don't have time, when she asks me if I can do the shopping. I always used to do it, she says. I don't answer. Tell her that I can't go out. She says that this writing's a strange notion. The playing was better after all, then. At least it was possible to talk to me when I was doing that, she says. It was this summer that I met Knut again. I hadn't seen him for many years, I can hardly remember when I last saw him, but we met this summer. And Knut had gotten married. Had two kids. I just sit here. I haven't amounted to anything. I met Knut this summer. I met him a couple of times, then I didn't see him again. I saw his wife a few times, she walked past along the road, she looked up at my house, but I don't think she saw me. I was hidden, inside the room. After the night when Torkjell and I played at the community dance, this notion that I didn't want to go out came over me. I haven't been outside a door since that evening. Knut dances with an old school friend. I don't know what it is. A restlessness has come over me, a terrible restlessness, I don't know what it is, but I can't bear this restlessness. It's only because of this restlessness that I write. I don't know. The day after Torkjell and I played at the community dance this summer, early in the morning, I stood out in the yard, I don't think I thought about anything in particular, not about Knut, not about his wife, I just stood there, didn't think about the night before, then I saw Knut, down on the road, he saw me, I waved, but he only shook his head lightly, and Knut thought that it was all a long time ago, he must've seen us, must know everything, and it shouldn't matter, but it was that time, that girl, don't want to anymore now, just must, can't, sees me standing there, must say, meet, do, and he can't but must, cannot, should, stands there, and he doesn't know, sees me, and now should, this too, must sleep a little, not say anything, must've seen it, he knows everything, Knut thinks, and then he stands there, down on the road, stands there and looks up at me. I didn't know what to do, I just stood there, and Knut just kept standing there down at the roadside, he just stood there, didn't do anything. I waved to him again, but now Knut didn't react, just stood there, at the roadside. I didn't know what to do, so I began to walk down toward the road, and then, at once, Knut began to walk out along the road, and Knut thought that now, no this won't do, should just walk, knows everything, must've seen us, this, must get away now, walk away to some place or other, can't just, must be able to, everything like, and now, this, it penetrates the face, gets stuck there, can't cry, not call, just is, must go, can't say anything, just thought, just walk, walk away, have nothing to say, tomorrow, not sleep, go home now, relax, not so important, must just say something, Knut thought, and I called out to him, but Knut didn't answer, just walked outward along the road. I stopped. I didn't know what to do. I remained standing on the road, and I saw Knut walking outward along the road. I stopped. I didn't know what to do. I remained standing in the road, and I saw Knut walking outward along the road, and Knut thought that now he walked, just walked away, doesn't know, must go, shall, go now, sleep, find something, like, cannot, walk, don't talk, a long time since we were small, the boathouse, walk past it, must've seen us, knows everything, and he doesn't want to, just has to walk, Knut thought, and I saw Knut walking outward along the road. Since that time I haven't seen Knut. It's this restlessness. I sit and write, don't go out. I hear my mother walking across the floor down there. My mother isn't very old. She strokes my hair. She says that I can't just sit inside, must go outside now and then. I'll become quite crazy from all this writing, she says. My mother. I hear her walking across the floor, hear the sound of the television. I don't know. Knut and me, we were always together, and

Knut just walked away, I watched his back. Knut dances with someone from his class. I sit here and write. I haven't touched the guitar since the restlessness came over me. I don't know.

It was this summer that I met Knut. For the first time
for at least ten years I saw Knut again. I came walking down
along the road, was going to the library, it was a fine summer's
day, a little late in the afternoon, and then, toward me on a
bend, I saw Knut appearing, first Knut and a few meters
behind him came his wife, Knut's wife, she was small, plump,
had black hair and brown eyes, and on each side of her walked
two little girls. I saw Knut coming toward me. I looked at
Knut, I saw him almost without looking at him, and he
looked at me, I lifted my arm, waved, we walk, approach each
other, and then Knut lifts his arm, we walk toward each other,
we wave to each other. Knut and I come closer and closer to
each other, and we wave carefully to each other, smile, and I
think that it's a long time since I've seen Knut, must be ten
years, it'll become difficult to see him again, I think, and
Knut probably thinks that he knew it, knew he had to meet
me again, meet other people he used to know, he has dreaded
it, doesn't know what to say, it's all so long ago, having a
holiday here, that's all they can afford, a long holiday, a music
teacher, it has to be here, can't afford to go anywhere else,
must be here, can't do anything else, and there, there I came
walking, a long time ago, many years ago, I came walking
toward Knut, and Knut thinks that he has to stop, must talk

to me, and we stop, stand next to each other on the side of
the road, talk, it's all right, we talk easily, so long since we
have seen each other, we say, and I ask if he wants to come
fishing with me, take a trip out on the fjord, and then one of
his daughters begins to nag him that he must come, has to
come now, and Knut says that they're going to the shop,
going to The Co-op, and I say that I'm going to the library,
and I say that we'll get together for a chat, and I nod to
Knut's wife, she nods back, she looks into my eyes, brown
eyes, and she looks calm, she looks into my eyes, and Knut
thinks that all he wants is to be left in peace, there's nothing
else he wants, and his wife looks at me like that, looks into
my eyes, he thinks, she's always like that, he thinks, looking,
and he just wants to be left in peace, that's all he wants, and
his wife looks at me like that, looks into my eyes, he thinks,
and I walk outward along the road, past the bend, out toward
the library, and Knut walks the other way, in toward The
Co-op and Knut thinks that he hopes he won't meet any
more people, doesn't know what to say, it's all so long ago.
Knut walks inland along the road. He stops, waits for his wife
and daughters, they catch up with him, and they walk inland
along the road together. They walk past a boathouse on the
downside of the road. Knut says that he played a lot in this
boathouse when he was a boy. His wife doesn't answer. She
keeps walking. Knut remains standing on the roadside
looking at the boathouse. He walks down to it, puts his hand
on the wall. He thinks that he has played a lot in this
boathouse, he and I together. We played a lot together. Knut
walks up again to the road, he sees that his wife has already

walked a fair way along the road, she would always look into people's eyes like that, putting on airs, he thinks, and he begins to walk, he walks behind his wife and kids, and he remembers how he and I, every day, after we'd come from school, were together, either he bicycled in to my place, or I bicycled out to his place, or we met in the boathouse, we bicycled together to and from school too, spent the lunch breaks together, and in the afternoon we were always together, first we played together, spent a lot of time in the old boathouse, and later it was the playing, the practice, the dances we played at, and that time we suddenly got the idea that we should start an orchestra, in the breaks, at school. Knut walks inland along the road, a few meters behind his wife, his daughters walk next to his wife, they hold her hands, a girl in each hand, the girls are skipping along the road. He turns and looks down toward the boathouse. It's a long time since he was home, he thinks. Why does he say home, he thinks. He's almost never here, is he, he thinks. Knut walks inland along the road a few meters behind his wife, he turns around again, looks down at the boathouse, and he thinks that he used to play there a lot, when he came from school it was straight home to get something to eat, then down to the boathouse, and if I wasn't already there, then I came after a little while, and he thinks about what we really did, what we were doing in the boathouse, he isn't sure, what was it really, perhaps nothing special, and Knut thinks that we were there, we made a secret room, up in the boathouse, that's where we spent time together. We collected things we found on the shore, mostly empty plastic bottles, driftwood, it could be the rest of a plastic toy, empty plastic bags, and what we found we carried up into the boathouse, sorted it, hid it, and otherwise we were there, hour after hour, we used secret names for each other, wrote messages with secret letters. Knut thinks that we were always there, now it seems so small, at the time it was so much, much bigger, it was big and secret. Knut walks inland along the road, he catches up with his wife, he tells her that he and I spent such a lot of time in the boathouse he showed her, and she says that he has said it already, and Knut says still, why shouldn't he say it, it's so strange to think about, now that he thinks back, everything seems so small, it was quite simply difficult to remember what we were doing, we collected trash on the shore, used secret names, different things like that, but at that time everything was so bountiful. His wife says yes, that's how it often is. They walk along the road, come to The Co-op. Knut feels shy when he walks in, it's so long since he has been there, he thinks. When he was a boy he was often there. Shopping for his mother. If he had a bit of money, he was there to spend it. Hadn't been there for such a long time. He goes in, and his girls begin to run around in the shop, his wife takes a shopping basket, and walks between the shelves. Knut walks next to his wife. He feels shy. The shop is exactly the way it always used to be. Nothing looks like it has changed. The smell is the same. Knut walks next to his wife in the shop, there are no other customers. A young girl sits in the cash register. They walk around in the shop. Just now and then does Knut get a glimpse of his girls. Knut thinks that he doesn't know the girl at the cash register, it's a young girl,

and there are no other customers in the shop, nothing much
to be afraid of, he thinks, isn't really all that dangerous, he
thinks, nothing to be shy about. They shop, pay, and they
walk out along the road again. Knut sees the boathouse and
he says it's really strange with this boathouse. His wife doesn't
answer. Knut says that it wasn't so bad to be at The Co-op as
he'd imagined, and his wife says that he must stop fussing
about everything, being worried, being shy about meeting
old friends, if that's how it is, why did he want to come here
for a holiday then, ha, they could've done something else in
the holidays, couldn't we, she says, and Knut doesn't answer,
keeps walking, and when they arrive home, his wife goes in,
his daughters stay outside, and Knut sits down at the garden
table, he sits and looks out over the fjord, it's a fine summer
afternoon, he hears his daughters running around laughing,
and Knut thinks that he has met me today, and of course his
wife had to look at me in that way, it's so long since we talked
to each other, Knut thinks, now he's married, has two kids, a
wife, has an education, a regular income, while I still live at
home with my mother, nothing has really happened to me in
all these years, he thinks, and I'm still the same as I once was,
live at home, have never lived anywhere else, well, I play the
guitar, play records, have begun to play at traditional dances,
must be because I need to earn a bit of money, Knut thinks,
and he thinks that he doesn't know what to say to me, it's all
such a long time ago, now everything's so different, like the
boathouse, which was so much, a whole life, almost, and
now there's nothing left, it's like that with most things, in
the end there's nothing left, it just disappears, everything

changes, and what once was becomes something very different to what it used to be, becomes smaller, becomes nothing, that's how it is, and there's nothing to do about it, it's just the way it is. Knut sits in his garden. His daughters are running around playing. After a while he goes into the house, he comes out again, holds a newspaper, and his sits down again on the garden bench. Knut thinks that he met me today, that I'm the same, nothing has happened to me, his wife looked me in the eyes in that way of hers, he thinks, she's always like that, and I asked if we should go out fishing together, go out on the fjord, he has never liked being out in a boat, fishing has never been his thing, Knut thinks, and he looks down toward the fjord, to the cove below the house, and he sees a boat gliding slowly along the shore, and that's me, he says, and Knut thinks that he doesn't want to go out on the fjord, has never enjoyed that, it's not his thing, and he sees the boat down there, a rowboat, with an outboard motor, the boat makes a few turns along the shore in the cove, before the boat gains speed, disappears mid-fjord, stops there a while, and then the boat disappears along the fjord. Knut sits in the garden, and he thinks that his wife looks at me in that way of hers. His wife comes out, she's properly dressed, in sea boots, rain clothes, and she says that she's going out on the fjord, she has talked to the neighbor, on the phone, she says, she could borrow the boat, that was no problem, if she knew how to use the outboard motor, she could use that too, there was petrol enough, a tank-full, she says, and Knut asks if she's going to fish, and she says that she is, there's a fishing rod and everything in the boat, but he didn't want to come with her, did he, he doesn't like to be on the fjord, she says, and Knut says that no, he doesn't, but she can go, on her own, but she must be careful, and she asks if he can help her with the outboard motor, she doesn't know how to use the motor, he must explain to her a little about the fishing gear too, he can do that, can't he, she says, and Knut says, of course he can, no problem, he says, and she asks him to come at once, she's ready, as he can see, she says, and she begins to walk down toward the shore, and Knut follows her, a few meters behind her, he walks behind her, down toward the shore, they walk along the shore, they cross the main road, she walks first, he follows, and then she stops, waits, asks where they should go, and Knut says that they'll just follow the main road a little inward, and then there's a path down toward the shore, and she begins to walk, sees the path, curving downward, she walks down a quarry, the path runs along a small brook, at the edge of a quarry, it's been a while since the meadow has been mowed in the quarry, and the grass has begun to grow out again. Knut's wife and Knut walk down toward the shore, she walks in front, he follows, they walk along a trickling brook. Knut pulls the boat, a fiberglass boat, in to land, climbs on board, he picks up a fishing rod lying in the boat, picks up a few fishing lures, explains to his wife how to use the equipment, how to cast the rod, change the lure, and Knut lowers the outboard motor into the water, and then he explains how to start the motor and he explains to her how to moor the boat. Knut goes ashore again, and his wife unties the boat, starts the outboard motor, the boat glides slowly out, she accelerates, the speed increases, and Knut sees her yellow rain jacket disappearing down the fjord, and then she turns quickly, she lifts her hand, she waves at him. Knut stands on the shore, and he waves back, before he begins to walk up the quarry again. Knut goes home, he sits down in the living room, turns on the television, unable to concentrate on what he's watching. His mother comes into the living room. She asks why he doesn't want to go fishing with his wife, why didn't he do that, she says. Knut says that he doesn't like to go out on the fjord. His mother sits down. She picks up her knitting. Knut looks at the television set, but he doesn't catch what he's watching. His mother asks if he wants some coffee, and Knut says that'd be good, and his mother goes to get two cups, a thermos flask, a tray of cookies. His mother says it's nice with children, with grandchildren, but it's certainly good when they've gone to bed, too. Knut says it's nice when the house's quiet. He looks at the television set. He isn't able to catch what he's watching. His mother says that he's got two good girls. Knut says that he's been lucky with them, yes. Knut stands up, says that he thinks he'll go for a walk, and his mother says why not, it's nice to go for an evening walk, she says. Knut goes out, looks at the fjord, but he can't see her boat. He walks along the road, past the boathouse, looks at the fjord, and he thinks that he met me today, hadn't seen me for many years, couldn't have seen me for at least ten years, we used to spend a lot of time together, played in a band, and today he met me again, it was strange, hadn't seen me for a long time, and he had dreaded it, has dreaded meeting me again, meeting other people again, he doesn't quite know what to say, it's such a long time ago, and his wife, and Knut thinks that his wife, she looked at me in that way of hers, now she's out on the sea, her yellow rain jacket, the black hair under the hood, her eyes, brown eyes, and Knut thinks that I asked if he wanted to come with him out on the fjord, we could do some fishing, and his wife heard it, that's why she's out on the fjord now, because she wanted to meet me, and I took a round into the cove below Knut's house, wanted to show her that now I go out fishing, had to get my speed up, drove in along the fjord, toward the small island, because didn't I say down on the road, when we met today, that I used to go to the small island, that it was there I went fishing. Knut walks inland along the road, and he thinks that his wife wants to go fishing because she wanted to meet me. He recognized the way she looked at me today. He knew what it meant. Knut walks inland along the road, and he thinks about the girl, the one at the dance where we played, it wasn't meant like that, not on his part. It was only a bit of fooling around on his part, and now perhaps I want to, can't be like that, he didn't mean anything improper, didn't think there was anything special about that girl, she was just an ordinary girl, but I became so strange after that, withdrew, became shy almost, didn't want to practice, only just turned up at the playing jobs, something happened to me, and Knut thinks that he doesn't know why, just thought she was an ordinary girl, nothing special, and then I became so strange, he still remembers it, not all that much he remembers from the playing jobs, from all those years when we were playing, but just that episode, that strange event, no, he doesn't quite know, something strange, doesn't quite know, something strange happened, something he can't quite understand, and Knut walks along the road, he looks out to the fjord, keeps going, he hurries, keeps going, doesn't quite know, he glances at the fjord, doesn't see anything, no boat to be seen, not my boat, not her boat, and Knut thinks that she rang the neighbor, asked to borrow his boat, and of course, that was no problem. Knut has arrived close up to the small island, and he stops, he stands at the roadside, and he sees two boats. There are two boats on the inside of the small island, and she sits in one of them, I sit in the other. The boats are lying close to each other. Knut stands on the roadside, and he looks out to the small island, and I turn around, see Knut, and I turn away, because Knut mustn't notice that I've seen him, that's how it is, Knut thinks, two boats lying out by the small island. Knut stands at the roadside, and he thinks that this, exactly, that's what he knew, it's always like this, he thinks, it's like this, the way she looked at me today, he should've known it, it's always like this, and Knut remains standing at the roadside, looks at us, and he thinks that he didn't mean anything by it, that time, at that dance, that girl, didn't know he'd done anything wrong, it just happened like that, nothing, and Knut looks out toward us, looks at the boats lying next to each other, and he begins to walk out along the road, he can't just stand there, Knut thinks, and he looks at the boats, two rowboats, one wooden, one fiberglass, two outboard motors, and Knut sees his wife leaning forward, her yellow rain jacket, and she smiles, his wife sits in the middle of her boat, and I sit in the middle of my boat,

we sit on the thwarts in the middle of the boats, and now he
sees it, he hasn't noticed it earlier, he sees that she has tied
her boat to my boat, and he sees that she smiles at me, we
talk together, she leans forward, she smiles, and Knut thinks
that he can't stand here, what if we see him, perhaps we've
already seen him, hadn't I looked up, looked toward land,
seen him, looked away again at once, yes I had, Knut thinks,
and he begins to walk inland along the road, he walks inland
along the road, better get home, he thinks, and he walks,
glances down at the fjord, and he sees me loosening the
hawser from her boat, it's tied around the thwart in the
middle of my boat, he sees me throwing the hawser over to
her, and she walks to the back of the boat, sits down at the
back, she tries to start the motor, the cord makes a cracking
sound, she tries again, another crack, and the motor starts,
and now she'll go home again, better get home now, Knut
thinks, and stops, he sees her turning toward the small island,
and Knut hears me starting my boat, and he sees me going
in another direction, and he sees me waving to his wife, she
turns her boat and follows my boat, and Knut thinks that
now we'll go ashore on the small island, now we're going to
hobnob in the heath, he thinks, and Knut laughs to himself,
and he begins to walk inland along the road, he walks fast,
and he laughs to himself, he'd better get home, he thinks, as
long as we haven't seen him, he thinks, but I have seen him,
I looked up, looked down again, I probably did see him, and
now we've gone ashore, we'll stay on the small island, it's
always like that, he noticed the way she looked at me today,
it was always like that. Knut walks inland along the road, he

has decided to go home, no reason for him to be standing on the roadside, and he walks inland along the road, and he thinks that now I and his wife are on the small island, had to happen, that girl at that dance, he didn't mean anything, but that's how it was, nothing to do about it now, and he walks inland along the road. Knut looks down at the fjord, he looks at a headland that stretches out into the fjord. He stops. Knut thinks that he wants to go down there, sit there and wait till we turn homeward, we've seen him anyway, he thinks, and Knut goes down to the headland, can he stay here, he thinks, it's just silly, sitting here and waiting for us, he remains staying there, sits down, it has started to become dark, and Knut thinks that he can't just sit here, it was just a bit of nonsense with that girl, the one at the dance, it's so long ago, how could he know, and I became so strange afterward, for a long time, nothing was the same anymore, didn't want to any longer, nothing was the same, I became so shy, didn't want to anymore, he didn't know, did he, couldn't know, could he, it just happened like that, how could he, he couldn't, wasn't possible, and Knut sits there and waits, he just sits there, has decided to stay sitting there, just sit there, he thinks, and he hears himself laughing, remains sitting there, and then he hears the sound of two outboard motors, he stands up, goes down to the headland, and then he gets a glimpse of my boat, me first, and a couple of boat-lengths after, rocking in the waves from my boat, comes her boat. Knut stands up down at the headland. He looks at me, and Knut lifts his hand and waves when I see him, and I wave to Knut, and Knut sees that my speed slows, I turn toward land, and Knut sees that his wife does the same. Knut watches me bringing my boat slowly in to land. First Knut says nothing, and he thinks that finally, he can get a ride in her boat on the way home, and then he says that he took an evening walk, says different things, and Knut climbs into his wife's boat, and she shows him the fish she got, that's dinner tomorrow, Knut says, and then he says bye, goes to the back of the boat, starts the outboard motor, and Knut doesn't look back when he steers the boat out on the fjord, and he thinks that finally, it's over now, and he asks if his wife has had a good time, ha, he's sure she has, and she doesn't answer, and he asks why she has to come on to me, if that's a good thing, why the fuck does she do that, he says, and she doesn't answer, why does she have to do it, Knut says again, and she doesn't answer, doesn't say a word, she sits on the thwart in the middle of the boat, she doesn't even turn around, doesn't answer, and Knut shakes his head, begins to laugh. Knut doesn't say anything else, steers the boat home, they've arrived, she walks ashore, walks up the quarry, homeward, he moors the boat, the cod is left in the boat, and Knut takes the fish, throws it into the sea, and the seagulls arrive immediately. Knut walks home, locks the door, goes to bed, and the wife is already in bed, and Knut says that she must calm down now, she says she wants to go to sleep, he must leave her alone now. Knut doesn't say any more, and the next day he wakes up late, it's already broad daylight. Knut thinks she'll have to stop this, can't keep it up like this, the way she looked at me, it shouldn't happen. Knut stays in bed for a long time, and he thinks that now, something must happen, she and I were at the small island, went ashore there, he must ask her what we did on the small island, find it out, it shouldn't happen, and that girl, the one at the dance, it's so long ago, and he didn't know, did he, not his fault. Knut stays in bed, stays there until one of his daughters comes and says that it's lunchtime, then he goes down, the others are already sitting at the table when he comes down, and his wife doesn't even look at him, neither she nor Knut speak a word to each other while they are eating. Knut thinks that he must question her, must know what she and I were doing on the small island. No one says anything. After lunch, Knut goes up to the bedroom again, lies down in bed, tries to read, and he thinks about what she and I did on the small island, he must ask her, that girl at the dance, it was just a bit of nonsense, it wasn't his fault, but I became so strange afterward, became quite shy, didn't want to practice anymore, but it's a long time ago. Knut lies in bed, and he thinks that he must ask her, find out, had dreaded to come here, meet old acquaintances, don't know what to say, he thinks, and his mother comes up, knocks on the door, enters, her head bowed, and she asks if he wants some coffee, and Knut says, thanks, that would be nice, he says, and he thinks that now he'll ask his wife what she and I did on the small island yesterday. Knut goes down to the living room. Only his mother is there. Knut asks where his wife is, and his mother says that she and the kids have gone for a walk, and Knut thinks that now she has gone to meet me, to see if she can see me, meet me along the road, she must have gone to The Co-op, he thinks, that's why she isn't here, he thinks, and after finishing his coffee, Knut says that he'll go and sit outside, and his mother says that she's sure to come soon, his wife, she has only gone for a walk, she says. Knut goes into the garden, sits down there, he has brought a book, tries to read. He thinks that his wife and kids are sure to come home soon, and then he must ask her, find out, what she and I did on the small island. Must ask her about it, he thinks. Knut hears laughter, and then he sees his girls come running up toward the house. A little while afterward his wife comes walking. Knut nods to her. She goes and sits down next to him. Knut asks, was it a nice walk, and she says, yes, it was, and then she asks if he has calmed down now, come to his senses again, she can't stand it if he's to be like this. Knut doesn't answer. She says that he'll have to stop this. Knut doesn't answer. His wife shakes her head, stands up, goes inside, and Knut thinks that he must ask her now, find out what she and I did on the small island, surely he can ask about that, and Knut decides, he'll ask her, and he goes inside, and he thinks that he has to ask, but he doesn't want to go into the living room, that dance, that girl, but it didn't mean anything, and he goes up to the attic, she won't answer him anyway, just says that he has to stop it, and Knut lies down on the bed again, tries to read. He thinks that he should be able to ask her, and Knut hears steps on the stairs, he hears laughter, and his wife comes up to the attic, she holds a daughter in each hand, and she says that he'll have to put the kids to bed tonight, it's his turn now. Knut thinks that he must get the kids to bed first, then he'll ask her, she looked at me in that way, he thinks, and Knut puts the kids to bed, reads to them, but they don't want to sleep, are not tired at all, and then he hears voices in the hallway, one of the girls jumps up in bed, and Knut says that she must lie down now, she sits up in bed, with big eyes, and she listens, once more Knut says she must lie down again, it's just someone talking, he says, and then the other girl sits up in bed, the girls look at each other, and Knut says that they must go to sleep, it's late at night now, he says. The oldest girl climbs out of bed, looks at Knut, then she goes to the door, opens it, looks at Knut again, and then she closes the door behind her, and then he hears her walking down the stairs, and Knut looks at the youngest girl, she's already about to climb out of bed, and Knut thinks that now, he hears the voices, now she has gone to get me, gone home to my place to get me, to bring me out here, he hears the voices, her voice, my voice, can only hear the voices, she has gone to get me, he thinks, gone home to my place, perhaps she has met me along the road, she has dragged me out here, he thinks, and Knut sees the youngest girl sneaking out the door, and he thinks that it doesn't matter, just as well that the girls are up now, it's evening, can't turn into anything anyway, suppose it must, that dance, he didn't mean anything, that girl, he didn't know, did he, didn't mean to make a pass at my girl, didn't know, did he, it's so long ago, something must happen now, can't just be sitting here, can't do that, must do something, go down, his wife is in the hallway, with me, surely something has to happen, must go down, but he doesn't want to, isn't able to, can't do it, and someone's calling, his name, calling, it's her calling, must come down, the caller says, must come down, and he isn't able to, must go down, and Knut stands up, walks toward the door, turns off the light, walks down

the stairs, and then he sees me, I'm standing there, just inside
the front door, I've taken off my shoes, but have still got my
jacket on, just like the old days, Knut thinks, everything's
like before, I stand there, furthest away in the hallway, I have
taken off my shoes, but I'm wearing my jacket, and Knut
doesn't see his wife, sees only me, as I'm standing there, and
everything's like before, he thinks, the way it was a long time
ago, and then his wife says something, but he doesn't hear it,
doesn't want to hear it, everything's like before, the way it was
a long time ago, I stand in the hallway, furthest away, without
shoes, but with my jacket on, and Knut smiles, with his whole
face, and he walks down the stairs, walks along the hallway,
and he says that I must come in, let's go into the living room,
he says, and Knut thinks that now everything is like before,
no nonsense anymore, everything is like before, smooth
sailing now, and Knut stands in the doorway to the living
room, he stands there, and he thinks that this is how it should
be, and his wife is in the living room, she calls something,
must ask her what she's doing, looked at me in that way, were
out on the small island yesterday, she and I, must ask her, find
out what it is, always like this, and he must say something to
his wife, answer her, cannot bear this, something has to
happen, and then Knut's mother puts her head through the
kitchen door, and Knut looks at her, she smiles, and once
more everything is like before, back to what it used to be,
nothing has happened, and then his mother claps her hands
together, it's all so long ago, his wife, she looks at me in that
way, is out in the boat with me, passes me up on the road,
walks home to my place, the girl at the dance, didn't mean

anything, Knut thinks, and he sees his mother clapping her hands together, hears that she says something, everything's so long ago, and Knut walks into the living room, everything's so long ago, is quite different now, and he thinks that he can't keep this up, must be an end to it, and he calls, and his voice is strangely hard, almost hard, he calls that his mother must come into the living room, too, and his voice is so hard, Knut thinks, and he walks over to the window, sits down in front of the window, he can't stand this, he thinks, and he leans his elbow on the windowsill, looks out of the window, he looks down into the bay and he sees the boat, she was out on the fjord yesterday, on the small island, she and I were on the small island, Knut thinks, and he thinks that he must ask her what we were doing there, ha, what the hell did we do there, and then Knut glances around, says something to me, and Knut thinks that he's just saying something, just has to say something quite ordinary, and Knut sees his wife sitting on the sofa, she leans aslant on one armrest, and Knut hears her saying something to me, must talk, in an ordinary way, about normal things, nothing special, and Knut hears himself saying something, doesn't quite notice what he's saying, just says something, and then I begin to talk about the community dance, tomorrow, I have to make a fuss about that, it's because I'm so proud that I'm going to play there that I make a fuss about it, it's always like that, wanting his wife to come there, and rather without him, that's why I must talk about the community dance again and again, just a bit of nonsense, nothing has become of me, and I don't do anything, play with an awful accordionist, and I'm proud of that, that girl at the dance, what happened, must, and then those infernal kids, should have been in bed a long time ago, she lies there on the sofa, legs apart, the kids are bellowing out in the hallway, an infernal noise, she lies there on the sofa, and I'm sitting in an armchair, in the middle of the room, behind Knut, and she lies there on the sofa, says that she'd like to go to the community dance, would like to hear me play, she says, and the kids are making a racket out in the hallway, and it's late now, they should've been in bed a long time ago, and Knut thinks that he can't stand this, must do something about it, and he stands up, better go into the hallway, calm them down, at least, he thinks, and he walks into the hallway, closes the door behind him, and he says to the girls that they must calm down, mummy'll be coming any minute, it's her turn to put them to bed tonight, he says, and the girls become quiet, walk over to the stairs, sit down on the lowest step, and they look at him, they must be quiet now, Knut says, and he thinks that she has to be showing up now, can't just sit there in the living room with me, surely she, too, must do something, he thinks, and Knut goes to stand in the doorway to the living room, he says that his wife really has to come and put the kids to bed now, and she stands up, smiles at me in that way and then she puts on airs, shrugs her shoulders, and then she comes walking, doesn't look at him at all, Knut thinks, just looks straight past him, says something about supposing it was her turn, says something about him enjoying himself, and Knut closes the door, goes in, he can't go over to the window, can't sit down here now, must talk to me, he thinks, he must talk in quite an ordinary way, talk about normal things, must sit down on the sofa, and Knut hesitates a little, and then he goes and sits down on the sofa, and I sit in the armchair, in the middle of the room, and I look out the window, and we say something, ordinary words, harmless words, Knut thinks, and he sees that I stand up, walk over to the window, I stand there, look out, and Knut thinks that now I'm looking at the fjord, at the boat his wife borrowed yesterday, now I'm thinking about her body, there on the small island, in the darkness, I see her boat, the boat she borrowed, but I look so calm, so that's not it either, Knut thinks, I just stand there and look, don't say anything, and Knut stands up, comes and stands next to me, looks out of the window, and everything is almost like in the old days, his wife isn't in the living room, it's just me and him, Knut thinks, some of the old things are in the living room, out on playing jobs, secret smoking, the parties, all the beer cases, after the playing jobs, sitting there with a bottle of beer each, and the girls who were left after the dance stood in front of the stage while the hall was emptied, until we had begun to disassemble the equipment, and Knut remembers that he has brought something to drink, perhaps he can offer me something to drink, he thinks, and we talk about the fjord, about being out fishing, and Knut says that can he offer me a drink, if I want one, he says, and then he goes to get the drinks, and Knut sits down in an armchair that stands in front of the window, and Knut watches me getting the armchair that stands in the middle of the room, and then we sit there next to each other, in front of the window, and Knut thinks that there has to be an end to this,

he can't stand it, it can't continue like this, it's half-dark in
the living room, he thinks, must turn on the light, and Knut
hears me asking if his wife has gone to bed, and he answers
something, I have to ask about his wife, obviously, he thinks,
and I sit there and drool, he thinks, and he doesn't think she
has gone to bed, he says, she'll come soon, he says, and he
thinks that I'm after his wife, he met me yesterday, on the
road, a long time ago since he last met me, must be, this can't
go on, and Knut hears me saying something, and then he says
that I haven't had a lot of women, have I, but we could meet
on the fjord, me and his wife, and Knut grins, empties his
glass, fills the glass again, and Knut thinks that he must say
something, he must tell him that he knows everything, his
wife has told him everything, must say something, and then
he says that I don't like to travel either, his wife has told him
that, he says, and after he has said that, everything changes
again, it seems, and Knut thinks that now we're talking
normally, the way one should talk, and then my voice is so
strange, Knut thinks, and then he must ask if I don't like to
work, and Knut thinks that that dance, that time, he didn't
know I was after that woman, how could he know that, ha, of
course he couldn't know that, and then Knut hears steps on
the stairs, he looks up, gets his glass, drinks up, and refills the
glass, and there are steps on the stairs, Knut hears them, and
he drinks, and his wife comes into the living room, it was
quick tonight he thinks, she really got the kids to bed in a
great hurry tonight, and now she looks at me in that way,
Knut thinks, and now she'll have a drink, too, she'll get a
bottle of wine, she says, now she'll fill her glass, thinks Knut,

now she'll begin, he thinks, and then he thinks that he can't
just sit here with me, without saying anything, must say
something, he thinks, and why don't I drink, come now, have
a drink, he says, ha, and Knut drinks, pours more whiskey,
his wife, now she'll fill her glass, flirt, look at me in that way,
he thinks, always like that, and his wife comes into the living
room, pushes her breasts forward, laughs, sways, and she
waves a water glass, a juice glass, says that there aren't any
proper glasses in the house, she must say, always like that,
Knut thinks, always like that, his mother, she'll be sitting in
the kitchen, she keeps to herself there, mostly, always has, but
now she almost never comes into the living room, not now
that they are there, his mother, there aren't any proper glasses
in this house, his wife says, can still drink wine, she says, and
his wife has sat down, slides into the corner, leans against the
armrest, pushes her breasts out, and she looks at me in that
way, and then she stands with her legs apart, lets her legs
glide slowly apart, her legs apart, mustn't, and everything
that should, finding the way to something, her legs apart,
puts the wine bottle between her legs, pushes the corkscrew
into the cork, and Knut looks at me, I look straight ahead,
out of the window, and Knut thinks that now she'll do
something exciting, show how tough she is, and Knut looks
at me as I stand up, looks at his wife, and he asks if he can
help her with the cork, and she answers no, and Knut thinks
that of course not, that's not on, that he, it's always like this,
must be like this, and then I stand up, of course, now we're
going to humiliate him, becomes so much better to fuck
each other then, oh yes, he understands that, that's the way

it is, and he watches as I open the wine bottle, and she sits there, legs apart, and his wife and I sit and smile to each other, making secret signs, we're laughing at him, Knut thinks, and he must say something, say that I must stop this, must leave his wife alone, damn it, and he says that I like his wife, don't I, and she likes me, he says, and she says that of course she likes me, she says that she's trying all she can to seduce me, the only thing that preoccupies Knut is that other men should fuck her, she says, that's how he is, she says, and Knut sits and looks out of the window, it's getting dark, his glass stands on the windowsill, and he hears me saying that I should be getting home, and Knut thinks that he isn't able to answer, just has to stay silent, not say anything, and then he turns around, looks at me, asks why don't I stay for a little longer, and Knut thinks why, is there a reason why he's asking that, why does he say that, and then he hears his wife saying something, that I have to stay or something like that, she says, and Knut has turned around again, he stares out the window, then he says again why don't I stay, there are drinks and women here, he says, why not stay, ha, he says, and now he can't be bothered anymore, he thinks, doesn't matter now, it makes no difference, it's all the same, doesn't matter what happened on the small island, she'll never tell him anyway, it's not a big deal, he'll just have some more whiskey, pure whiskey, and let everything get a bit numb, just let her stand there behind him, clinging to me, smooching with me, that's what she wants, it doesn't matter, damn it, she can just keep going, can do what she wants, fuck it, it makes no difference, can just keep going, let her smooch as much as she likes,

Knut thinks, and then he turns around, and Knut sees his wife standing there with one arm around my back, leaning into me, and in the other hand she is holding her glass, she can just keep going, Knut thinks, and then he looks at me, and then he says that's how his wife is, if only she'd been drunk, but she isn't, that's the way she is, he says, and Knut hears me saying I'd better be getting home, and Knut turns and sees me walking into the hallway, and he watches his wife walk toward him, and she sits down in the other armchair in front of the window, and Knut thinks, what does she want, what's going to happen now, and then he says, what does she really want, what's she after, and Knut sees me putting my head through the door, and he hears me saying that there's a community dance tomorrow, perhaps I'll see them then, Knut hears me saying, and Knut thinks that I don't want to let go of his wife, wants to smooch with her tomorrow too, he thinks, and then Knut sees me walking out the door, he hears me closing the door, and then Knut turns to the window, and he stares at the window, and he says, loudly, without turning around, that he doesn't understand what she wants, what she's after, he says, and he looks out of the window, and it's getting dark now, he notices, his features are clearly reflected in the windowpane, and Knut lifts his glass, toasts himself, his own mirror reflection, and his wife sits in an armchair next to him, in front of the window, and she asks what he's doing, doesn't he have anything else to do, she asks, and Knut doesn't answer, drinks more whiskey, and Knut doesn't say anything, and his wife stands up, gets the wine bottle, and then she says no, there's no point in sitting here, she'll go to bed, she says, and Knut could, if he can be bothered, try to push the cork back in the wine bottle, it's half-full, she says, and then she puts the glass on the coffee table, walks toward the door, leaves the door ajar, and Knut hears her walking up the stairs. Knut looks out of the window, he leans back in the chair, puts one foot on the edge of the windowsill. He looks out of the window, it's almost dark now and the whole room is reflected in the window. Knut thinks what should he do now, and he notices that he's tired, and his mother, she just went to bed, didn't even pop her head inside the living room, she heard me in the hallway, and then she showed her face, and later, where has she been, what has she done, hasn't shown her face. Knut empties his glass, he stands up, and he sees the half-empty wine bottle standing on the table, and he thinks that he'd better tidy up, he should carry the bottles and the glasses into the kitchen, he thinks, is tired now, he'd better go to bed, is tired, and what should he do with the wine bottle, must empty it, he thinks, and then Knut goes into the kitchen, empties the rest of the wine in the sink, throws the bottle in the rubbish bin, carries out the water jug and the glasses, puts the armchair that had been moved over to the window back to its place in the middle of the room, next to the round table, then he turns out the light in the living room, takes the whiskey bottle with him, walks up the stairs, and before he goes into the room where he and his wife sleep, he looks into his daughters' room, they're sleeping heavily, the oldest has kicked her doona half off, and Knut goes and spreads the doona over her, before he goes into the room where he and his wife sleep, the light is

turned off, and Knut doesn't want to turn it on, that could
wake his wife, in case she's sleeping, and he can't stand the
thought of that, must be left in peace now, he thinks, can't
bear any more now, and Knut notices that he's calmer now, is
not drunk, just a bit calmer, more tired, he wants to go to bed
now, sleep, and Knut undresses, crawls into bed, as far away
from his wife as he can come, and Knut drifts into sleep, and
the next day, when he wakes up, he's alone in the bed, he
feels under the weather, his forehead is warm. Knut stays in
bed, finds a book, tries to read, and then he hears someone
running on the stairs, light feet up the steps, and then he
sees his oldest daughter in the doorway, and she says that
he'll have to get out of bed now, is he going to stay in bed all
day, it's time to get up now, grandma has finished making
lunch, the girl says, and Knut says yes, he'll get up now, he'll
come down in a minute, and then the girl disappears, and
Knut gets out of bed, dresses, and goes down. Knut walks
into the kitchen, and the others are sitting around the table
already. He sits down, and his mother says that he keeps late
mornings. His wife sits there, and she doesn't look at him,
just sits there, again, now it'll start again, Knut thinks, they've
been here a couple of days, and it doesn't let up, Saturday
today, community dance, and soon she'll ask if they should
go to the community dance, surely he wants to go too, she'll
say, if Knut doesn't want to go, she'll drop in anyway, she'll
say, she'll go regardless, and then she'll say that she'll go for
a walk, she'll walk inland along the road, and Knut knows
that she'll go to meet me, and Knut's going to ask what she
was doing on the small island, he'll have to stop this, she'll

say. Knut sits at the end of the kitchen table, and he doesn't say anything, no one's talking, not even the girls. After the meal, Knut says he'll go into the garden, wants to do a bit of reading, he says. Knut goes out, and after a while his wife comes out with the daughters. She says that they want to go for a walk, perhaps drop into The Co-op, buy ice cream for the kids, and she asks if Knut wants to come. He says he doesn't feel like it, would rather sit here, wants to read a bit, he says. Knut watches his wife and kids walking along the road, and he thinks that now she'll go, she'll meet me now, that's all she wants, that's all she's after, just one thing she wants, nothing else, always the same, why should it be any different, and tonight, the community dance, and I'm going to play the guitar, accordion and guitar, traditional dance, doesn't want to go, but she'll want to, must go. Knut sits in the garden, and he tries to read. He can't concentrate. And he puts the book aside. Knut thinks that now his wife is going there to look for me, walking slowly along the road, wanting to meet me, she has the kids with her, she took the kids with her just for show, and Knut sees his wife coming, she's holding a girl in each hand, she smiles at Knut, says this is a fine summer's day, she has bought some sweets for the kids, she says, it's Saturday night, they're staying at home with their grandma while she and Knut go to the community dance, they have to have some sweets then, she says, and Knut nods, the kids go inside, and his wife sits down on the bench next to Knut, and Knut doesn't quite know what to say, he can't ask what she did on the small island now, impossible, and she says that they have to go to the dance, at least drop in, have a look, and Knut nods, says they probably should, and then she says that he mustn't be so reluctant about everything, he mustn't, it doesn't matter if he meets people he hasn't seen for many years, why worry about what he's going to say to them, no one else worries much about it, she says, and Knut doesn't answer, then she stands up, goes inside, and Knut picks up his book again, tries to read. Knut sits in the garden, trying to read. He can't do it, can't concentrate, and he goes up to the attic, lies down on the bed, he nods off, and he sleeps until his wife calls that he must wake up now, the girls are asleep now, she says, and if they're going to that community dance they'd better get ready and get going, the dance has already started, she says, and Knut gets up from the bed, rubs the sleep from his eyes, his body feels soft and tired, he doesn't answer at once, and his wife says that she'll go fetch some clothes, go down, she'll get ready first, and the bathroom should be available in a few minutes, he can lie in bed and stretch until then, she says. Then she leaves. Knut gets up, dresses, and he thinks that he won't be able to go to the community dance, they'll all be there, all the old acquaintances, he doesn't want to, doesn't know what to say to them, but his wife, she wants to go, there's nothing else lor it, he'll have to come, go home again almost immediately, go out and turn back again, almost, he thinks, and Knut takes a swig of the whiskey, waits a little, takes another swig, and then he decides to take the bottle with him, it was always like that in the old days, and that's how it'll be tonight, he thinks, and Knut walks down the stairs, down to the hallway, finds his jacket, puts the bottle in the inner pocket, and then he sits in the hallway, waiting for his wife, she comes, and then Knut calls to his mother that they're leaving now, going to the dance, and just as he calls, without having thought about it, it occurs to him that it has always been like this, he's called just like this many a time, but that was a long time ago, and now, suddenly, for a very short while, it's not very long ago, now it's sort of the way it has always been, the way it was many years ago, something's happening, and his mother opens the living room door, smiles, and she says have a good time, won't you, she's too old for things like that now, she says, and then Knut and his wife leave, they walk along the road, they walk next to each other, silently, and Knut thinks that he can't stand this, he understands why she's so keen to go to the community dance, not difficult to understand, she wants to see me on the stage, watch me play, be able to stand there and watch me, and then, afterward, she wants me and her to be together, that's the way it is, and that dance, that girl, he didn't mean anything, and I became so strange afterward, became shy, didn't want to practice anymore, I only just turned up at the playing jobs, and Knut thinks how could he possibly know, she was just an ordinary girl, if he sat and talked and fooled around a little with her, so what, ha, didn't mean anything, meant nothing, how could he know, Knut thinks, and now he must meet people he hasn't seen for many years, must talk to them, ask what they're doing, tell them what he's doing, and why must he always be so embarrassed, and his wife, meeting me, playing traditional dance, why does he always have to be so embarrassed, couldn't, can't stand this, Knut thinks, and he takes out the bottle, takes a swig, they keep walking, and they come down a large hill, and the valley opens, the road goes around a bay, out to the Youth Hall, and then Knut is in the Youth Hall, it's fully lit up, a few people are standing outside, there are rows of cars along the road, the party is in full swing, Knut thinks, and they walk out toward the Youth Hall, neither Knut nor his wife speak, they just walk. Knut thinks that this, he cannot bear this, doesn't quite understand why, he should never have come, he just follows her, can't stand it, and they've arrived at the Youth Hall, and Knut sees that there are people gathered on the platform in front of the Youth Hall, many people, and he must pass them quickly, mustn't talk to anyone, mustn't look at anyone, and his wife walks a little behind him, a couple of meters, and Knut hurries up, walks through the door, into the hallway, he walks over to the ticket window, and he doesn't know the girl who's sitting there, and Knut buys tickets, he notices his wife standing behind him, right behind him, and he turns around, gives her one of the tickets, and then they walk toward the entrance, and Knut sees that the hall is almost full, and then he hears the music, and he looks at the stage, and he sees me standing there, a little to the right, a little behind the accordion player, and Knut sees me strumming and strumming the chords, the same grating sounds, same chords, and Knut thinks that this is how it is when you play a waltz, the same one again and again, and then Knut notices that his wife is pushing him from behind, he hands in his ticket, walks inside, and Knut thinks that I'm standing in the same place I always have, a little toward the back of the stage, a little to the right, seen from the hall, and now almost everything is the way it was, Knut thinks, he has stood on that stage many times, incredibly many times, he thinks, hour after hour, and it was a cold, empty hall, an electric heater on one side of the stage, and his fingers were stiff, and then they had to play, learn new tunes, play the same old repertoire, and there I stand now, the way I've always stood, but now I play traditional dance, Knut thinks, and he notices that his wife's standing close to him, she'll cling to him now, he thinks, she was the one who absolutely wanted to come here, if it had been up to him, he can't stand all this, people he used to know, must talk to them, ask, tell, and there right in front of him, a girl he used to go to school with, she has become a woman, filled out, her hair is short, curly, she comes toward him, and she smiles, well, it's been so long, many years, so much has happened, she says, and Knut doesn't know what to say, to do, says that yes, it's been a long time, too long, and then she says something about him having a family now, kids, something about his wife, and Knut thinks he'll have to find something to say, what about a dance, he asks, and she nods, after so many years, yes, they have to have a dance, she says, it's not as if they dance together every day, oh no, she says, has hardly happened before, has it. Knut puts his arms around his old school friend, she puts her arms around him, and then they waltz, they glide around in the hall, it's a long time since he has danced traditional waltz, but he can still do it, he leads his old school friend firmly around in the waltz, they dance effortlessly, it's easier than Knut would've thought, and he looks down toward the door, looks for his wife, and she stands there, and Knut keeps dancing, then he sees his wife, she is talking to an elderly man, down by the exit door, and Knut says to the woman he's dancing with that there's his wife, the one standing by the door, and the woman he dances with says that's her husband, he's talking to Knut's wife, she says, and then Knut smiles, and they keep dancing. The waltz has finished and Knut says that it was good to dance an old waltz, it's been a long time since he'd done that, and his class friend says that they can do the next dance, too. Knut says that he'd like to very much, and then he says that he hasn't seen me playing since we were doing it together, the woman he's dancing with says that she has, and then she laughs a little, well that's our musician, she says, it's not really a proper dance unless I'm on the stage, she says, and then she laughs, and Knut's about to say something, but the music starts up again, it's a couple dance now, and Knut gets to say, before he surrenders to the dance, that this is more than he can do, but his class friend just waves it aside, and then they're under way, and Knut thinks that he can do it, indeed, no, he hasn't forgotten it, and then he glances at the door, for his wife, but he can't see her. Knut dances, and while he's dancing he's trying to lay eyes on his wife, and then he sees her, at the very front, on the bench, she's sitting alone, and she looks up toward me, and her eyes are warm. Knut dances, he tries to concentrate on the dance, and he dances, looks at his wife, and she sits alone on the bench, looking up at me. The dance has finished, and Knut thanks his old class friend for the dance, says he wants to go out for some fresh air, this kind of thing can be exhausting, not

every day, oh no, gets all sweaty, he says and then he walks to
the door, gets his ticket, walks out, and Knut thinks that he
mustn't look to the side, not look at anyone, he doesn't want
to meet anyone, and his wife, she sits there on the bench at
the front, alone, sits on the long bench that goes along the
whole wall, and she looks at me, sits there and looks at me,
and Knut thinks that he must go out, doesn't want this, it was
nice to dance, nice to meet his old school friend again, but he
doesn't want this, his wife, don't look at anyone now, and
Knut has come outside, and he has started to walk along the
road, he walks fast, walks past the row of parked cars, walks
fast, empty cars, should never, but no, she can't just sit there,
can't be like this, not possible, and Knut walks inland along
the road, doesn't want to meet anyone, has caught a glimpse
of several known faces, has looked away, doesn't want to
meet anyone, get away, go home again, no point in this, that
dance, that girl, can't understand, he didn't know, did he, and
now, must go back into the hall again, find his wife, take her
home, can't just walk along the road like this, and Knut stops,
makes up his mind, turns, and then he walks fast and reso-
lutely back to the hall, doesn't want to any more now, he
thinks, must get home now, he thinks, and he walks past the
group gathered on the platform in front of the Youth Hall,
some look at him, and someone calls, calls his name, but
Knut takes the stairs in two bounds, and he hurries through
the hallway, he hears someone calling behind him, but he
keeps going, pretends not to hear it, hands in his ticket, walks
into the hall, looks around, looks quickly at the faces, and he
doesn't see his wife, and then he walks forward, she's no

longer alone on the bench up there, and Knut takes a round around the hall, it's full now, people everywhere, heavy smell of tobacco, and he makes his way through the hall, he bumps into people who are dancing, but he doesn't see her, the house is full now, and Knut doesn't see his wife, and then he comes up with the idea that he should go to me, ask if I've seen her, and then he's sure, she's with me, he knows where she is, perhaps she's behind the stage, he knows where she is, Knut thinks, and he looks at me, he can see in my face that I know where she is, and Knut makes his way forward, to the edge of the stage, waves to me, he asks if I know where his wife is, and Knut sees me hesitating a little, then I shake my head, and then Knut says that she's probably gone home, and he thinks that she's with me, he knew it, he's sure of it, Knut thinks, and then he takes another round around the hall, and Knut thinks there's no point in doing it, but he still does it, he can't, he does it so I'll see him, believes that I don't know where his wife is, he thinks, and he walks around the hall, should be getting home, what's the use of this, just go home, no point, and Knut notices the eyes of the woman he danced with, she looks at him, doesn't want to look, go home, go now, don't look around, get away, he walks toward the door to the man who stands there and takes the tickets, but Knut doesn't take one, keeps going, walks through the hallway, mustn't look to the side, gets outside, they stand there, look at him, and then Knut hears someone saying that isn't it, yes, it is, such a long time ago, he's a music teacher, yes, they knew he'd end up doing something with music, and then they go silent, and Knut says it was good to see them again, must be getting home, yes, he'd better, but it's been a long time, they say, must take the trip home more often, they say, must keep in touch, they say, and Knut says yes, that'll probably happen, more often from now on, he says, and then he goes, says bye, and Knut leaves, he walks quickly down the road, must be getting home, perhaps his wife has gone home, she must have, he thinks, she's sure to have gone home, must have, with me, she's with me, behind the stage, that's why she wanted to go to the community dance, no other reason, only that, wanted to see me, Knut thinks, and he walks, has passed the row of cars now, homewards, met class friends, a group outside the Youth Hall, class friends, a long time ago, not so difficult to meet them, almost like before, get going, that girl, that dance, didn't mean anything, get away, I became so strange, embarrassed, didn't want to practice anymore, get home now, and Knut hurries along the road, has totally forgotten the whiskey, he thinks, almost hasn't been drinking at all, and then he pulls out the bottle, takes a swig, keeps going, hurries homeward, must get home, his wife is sure to be at home, Knut thinks, must be, didn't mean anything, just wanted to, and Knut sees his house, the house is dark, must be quiet now, mustn't wake his mother, he thinks, and he opens the front door carefully, walks up the stairs to the attic, into the bedroom, his wife isn't there, takes a look at his daughters, they're asleep, he knew it, it had to be like that, Knut thinks, doesn't know what to do, go down, think of something, and Knut walks quietly down the stairs, he must go out, he thinks, sit outside, wait, his wife's with me, he thinks, she sits behind the stage, sits there, must go out, wait, sit in the garden, wait, she'll come soon, and what are we doing, this isn't possible, must, and Knut sits in the garden, it's chilly, he pulls his jacket tighter around his body, notices the bottle in the inner pocket, he takes a swig, puts the bottle down on the ground, crosses his arms, presses them against his chest, and now the cars have started to come from the community dance, she'll come soon, he thinks, is with me, sits there behind the stage, that girl at that dance, it was nothing, he couldn't know, things like that happened often, didn't mean anything. Knut sits in the garden, he crosses his arms, presses them against his chest, bends his upper body. Knut watches as car after car drives past on the road, and he thinks that she'll be coming soon, she must come now, and he catches himself watching her in his mind walking quickly up the road, and then Knut thinks that she says, a little out of breath, that she's been looking for him all evening, what happened to him, just did a runner, did he, she couldn't find him, and then Knut imagines hearing her voice, down by the road, and he sits very still, and Knut thinks that no one must see him, it's dark, no one needs to see him, must just sit still, she'll be coming now, he thinks, she'll be with me, we're holding hands, we stop, she kisses my cheek, and Knut hears steps down on the road, there are two people coming, now he's certain, and then he hears her voice, it's her voice, but what she says, no that he can't hear, it's only her voice he can hear, and Knut sits still, and then he hears her saying that she'll walk a little further at least, no one answers, she wants to go with him, she says, doesn't want to go home, and she says that surely she can walk with me along the road, surely she can do that much, and Knut hears that I don't answer, don't say anything, and Knut grins to himself, shakes his head lightly, this is too silly, he thinks, can't be bothered, he thinks, it's enough now, and then he hears her saying that she wants to be with me, she doesn't want to go home, she says, and Knut becomes aware that this won't do, is too silly, can't continue like this, just must, and Knut stands up, slowly, and he walks down the hill, he walks down to the edge of the road, stands and looks along the road, and he hears his wife and I walking along the road, and then we stop, by the boathouse, and Knut thinks that no, surely we can't, didn't know anything about it, couldn't, has to, and his wife was sitting behind the stage, and I said I didn't know where she was, that's how it was, Knut thinks, and he can hear that she says something, he can't hear what it is, she'll probably be saying that they can't go to her place, my mother's there, they'll have to go somewhere else, she'll be saying, and I'll say that the boathouse, perhaps we can go into the boathouse, and then, at the same time, she'll be stroking my stomach, down toward the fly, and then Knut hears feet shuffling through grass, now we're going down to the boathouse, he thinks, and there, he'll have to get inside, Knut thinks, surely can't, nothing can, this isn't really all that far, must get there, is it, should be, and then Knut hears a few worn-out hinges squeak, now I probably open the side door, the hatch, he thinks, a long time since the door has been opened, must've been when we were kids, no one has opened it, doesn't think so, is something happening, it should, a long time ago, it could, and now we'll go into the boathouse, climb up the ladder, light the candle, and then we'll fuck, have to, yes, Knut thinks, nothing else than, have to get inside now, do, must, nothing else, should, it just must, like that, yes, fucking now, have to, like that, yes, is a music teacher, doesn't want to meet anyone, is shy, embarrassed, met people again, school friends, something happening, and now we're lying up in the boathouse, on the bench there, made from seine, old rotten cotton seine, in a sack, flour sack, and now we're fucking, Knut thinks, surely can't be, doesn't want to think about it, must get inside, doesn't know, well, just must, can't, happens, must, just can't, and Knut goes up again to the garden bench, sits down on the bench again, remembers the whiskey flask, takes a swig, crouches down again on the bench, it's cold, she'll come soon now, he thinks, it must be finished now, the community dance, now she'll soon come, he thinks. Knut is crouching, waiting, and he thinks that something must be happening, fucking, can't, as much as, this cold, just sits, it's too silly, sleep, everyone's asleep, and she sat at the back of the stage, inside the boathouse, up there, what happens, must be doing something, doesn't know, something couldn't just happen, can't, something must happen, and then Knut hears the sound of steps on the road, and he thinks that this, no more now, couldn't, just has to happen, should, late, cold, just has to sit here, then he hears obvious steps on the road, more obvious now, quick steps, and then he sees her, up on the road, she's walking with quick steps up the road, and she doesn't see him, Knut thinks, she hurries over to the front door, opens the door, walks inside, no point in this, Knut thinks, has to ask what she did, that night, out on the small island, must find out, he thinks. Knut sits crouched on the bench, he doesn't do anything else now, he thinks, just sit, nothing else, just now, find back, nothing else, he thinks, and after a while Knut sees his wife coming out on the porch, she stands and looks out, walks into the yard, looks down at the road, and then Knut says that yes, he's here, he sits here, he says and then his wife comes walking toward him, she walks up to him, and then she says that Knut should go to bed now, and Knut says that yes, it's bedtime now, it's late, he says, and then his wife goes in, and Knut picks up the bottle, goes inside, locks the door behind him, and then he walks up the stairs, takes a look at his daughters, he can see they're fast asleep, and then he walks into the bedroom, he can see that his wife's already in bed, and he puts the bottle away in the closet, undresses, ducks under the doona, and Knut notices that his wife pretends to be asleep, but he can't be bothered now, doesn't want to anymore, he thinks, and Knut ducks down in his bed, it's cold, but he's soon warm, and he doesn't know, Knut thinks, dozing, doesn't sleep properly, lies there, thrashes, his forehead's warm, and he lies there, and then he decides to get up, wants to take a walk, he doesn't want to anymore, Knut thinks, no more now, he gets out of bed, and then he dresses, and then he walks down the road, and he doesn't want to anymore now, he thinks, walks along the road, and then he looks at the house where I live, he sees me, I'm standing in the yard, and I wave to him, but now he doesn't want to anymore, Knut thinks, no more now, he thinks, just doesn't want to, it's not so important, doesn't want to, and then he sees me coming down the road and then Knut thinks that he has to get going now, must go now, he can't, it's impossible to talk, must go now, it's finished now, no more, must get some peace, just can't, not talk now, just not, no more, shouldn't, cannot, must, peace now, relax, not now, just doesn't want to, early in the morning, always people, no more now, not, Knut thinks, and then Knut begins to walk along the road, and he thinks that he'd better be getting home, yes he should, hurry, come, not now, wants some peace now, this is too silly, can't, music teacher, had to, not now, don't look, early in the morning, cold, can't, must, no more, finished, find the way back, is tired, should've been asleep, must, Knut thinks, and I see Knut walking along the road, and I think that this won't work, something terrible is going to happen, the restlessness is great, my left arm aches, my fingers. I stand and watch Knut walking along the road, I see his back, and later I have often seen him in my mind where he's standing down on the road, seen how he turns around, how he begins to walk down the road, seen his back. I sit here and write, and I don't go out anymore. A restlessness has come over me.

III

I just sit here, every day. I write to keep the restlessness at bay. I don't know if the restlessness has become bigger or smaller. I sit here and write. My mother walks across the floor downstairs, and I hear the sound of the television up here. Knut's wife. A yellow rain jacket. Denim jacket. Her eyes, my mother. She's not very old, strokes my cheek. She walks across the floor down there, and I can hear the sound of her steps up here. I hear the sound of the television. This won't do, she says. Must stop this writing. Must go out. I used to go shopping at least, now and then there were playing jobs. This won't do, she says. I don't go out anymore, I haven't touched the guitar since the restlessness came over me. I haven't done any more playing jobs, no more practicing either. I don't know. My mother. I must stop this writing, my mother says. After all, the guitar was better, she says. I sit here and write. I don't know. It was this summer that the restlessness came over me. I must keep the restlessness at bay. That's why I write. My mother walks across the floor down there, and I sit here and write. I have two rooms up in the attic, one of them can't really be called a room, it's almost a closet. The slanted ceiling makes it difficult to stand upright. I have my bed there. The bed is the only thing in the room. I use my bed a lot. It's this restlessness. I don't read anymore, all I do now is writing. I often used to go to the library. Since the restlessness came over me I don't read anymore. I don't know. I write, and then I go to bed. I don't go out anymore. It's this restlessness. This summer I met Knut and Knut walked away, I called, but Knut just kept walking. I often lay in my bed. In my bedroom, there's almost always a brown curtain drawn in front of the window. I don't go out anymore. It's this restlessness, my left arm aches, my fingers. I don't know. I haven't made anything of myself, and I'm more than thirty years old. Have no education, have never had a permanent job. I met Knut again this summer. Knut has become a music teacher, has got himself a family. Two daughters. Knut's dancing with someone from his class. I sit here and write, and I have a few books, a few records. I don't listen to the records anymore. I haven't touched the guitar since I started to write. I write to keep the restlessness at bay. I hear the sound of the television downstairs, I hear my mother walking across the floor, that's all. It's this restlessness. I met Knut again this summer, it must be ten years since I last saw him, then he comes toward me, on a bend. He has gotten married. Has two daughters. Knut's wife. I met Knut again. It was then the restlessness came over me. It was then I began to write. Knut and I. We got a band together, with a couple of others, a boy's band, we became older, began to play at dances all around the place, it was Knut and me, year after year, we were practicing, got playing jobs, early Saturday afternoon we would carry out our equipment, load it into an old van, then we'd drive a few hours to some Youth Hall or other, perhaps the organizers were already there, most often they were not, and then we had to make a call, drive around in an unfamiliar village, find the person who had the keys to the Youth Hall, before we could start carrying again, carry loudspeakers and guitar cases across the floor in a dark Youth Hall, up to the stage, lift it up on the stage, and then unpack it, adjust the sound, tune the guitar and the bass, then we had to rehearse a couple of songs, and then everything should be ready and we could sit down behind the stage with a beer and a smoke, sit and wait, take a few rounds on the stage, outside the Youth Hall, and there she was, one evening, she stood outside the Youth Hall, waiting for the dance to begin, stood there with a girlfriend. I saw her standing there. I walked in again, walked up on the stage, sat down behind the stage, I knew I'd seen her, she stood there, in front of the Youth Hall, stood there and waited for the dance to begin. I sit behind the stage, and Knut takes a round out on the stage, comes back and says that there are quite a few people here now, it's already fifteen minutes past the time, so we'd better get going, he says. I and the others finish the rest of the beer, stub out the smoke, we go out on the stage, and I pick up the guitar, check the tuning, it's good, I find the plectrum, wait for the others to finish theirs, and then we're ready, stand there, waiting for Knut to look around, and Knut looks at us, nods shortly, and then we get down to it, are never quite harmonized at the beginning, and I glance out in the hall, and the first people have already arrived, a few people have already arrived, and I look for the girl I saw standing outside the Youth Hall, the girl who stood there with a girlfriend, but I can't see her, a few girls, and few boys, line up in front of the stage, the first ones have begun to walk across the floor, a few girls have already sat down along the wall, I stand there and strum my chords, look around the hall. A few boys line up in front of the stage, stand there and admire the equipment. Weekend after weekend the same, again and again, playing jobs every Saturday night, different Youth Halls, and always the same. And then this time, that girl, she stands in front of the stage, I see her standing there. And then this one time, that girl, her eyes. She stands with her girlfriend in front of the stage, and I notice that she looks at me, looks away again, and I don't dare to look at her, to catch her eyes. I stand there, strum my chords. A group of boys are standing in front of the edge of the stage, admiring our equipment, saying something to each other, with their mouth close to the ear of the one they're talking to. And she stands there, with a girlfriend, and I don't dare to look at her, to catch her eyes. I strum and strum my chords. The first songs sound a little uneven, and we test them out, adjust the sound, they become more harmonized as the evening progresses. She stands in front of the stage. I see her standing there, she looks at me, and I look away, don't dare to catch her eyes. The hall begins to fill up, the sound is improving, the dance has got started, and she stands there in front of the stage, stands there with her girlfriend, just stands there. People are drifting in. Knut sings, announces the songs. On the whole we have a set order, a few changes now and then. In between two numbers, the odd person walks up to the stage, bends forward, asks us to play this or that tune, almost always the tune that's popular just then. If it's a tune we've practiced, now and then Knut says then we'll play it at once, now and then that it'll come later. We play. The hall fills up, more or less, only rarely does it become totally full. There are almost never just a few people. We play. She stands there in front of the stage, she looks at me, then she looks down. We play. We have a break, I put the guitar away, turn off the amplifier, walk behind the stage, find a beer, have a smoke. We're having a break and I put down the guitar, see that she's still standing in front of the stage, talking a little with her girlfriend now. Almost all playing jobs are the same, but then she was suddenly there. All weekends are almost the same, one year after the next. And then she's standing there. We're having a break, I sit behind the stage, and then I glance out into the hall, some people have started to stagger a little, others stand steadily and talk. That time, that girl, her eyes, something strange drawing me. New round. Get going. Number after number. A few people have gathered in front of the stage, they look at us. She stands there, with her girl-friend, and she looks at me, but I look away, don't dare to catch her eyes. People are dancing. A few people are lurching around the hall. Every Saturday night, week after week. That one time, that girl, her eyes, there she stands in front of the stage, stands a little bent, small, big eyes, glances up beneath her fringe, rests her weight on one foot, and around her people are dancing, shoving her, she moves a little, stands there again, the way she stood before. She stands in front of the stage, next to a girlfriend, looks at me, and then I decide that I, too, should look at her, and I look at her, she looks at me, and our eyes meet, and give way, everything happened

so quickly, and now we were there. We play, I stand there
with my guitar, strum my chords, I look out in the hall, and
she stands there, in front of the stage, and then I see quite an
inebriated fellow walking over to her, asking her to dance,
she shakes her head, and the fellow shrugs his shoulders,
walks away. We play. I strum my chords, Knut sings. She
looks at Knut, he looks at her. She stands in front of the stage,
with a girlfriend, and now I notice that she's looking at Knut,
not at me any longer, and Knut's looking at her. We play. She
stands there. Number after number. Knut looks at her all the
time. I strum my chords. We're having another break, and I
walk behind the stage, see that she remains standing in front
of the stage even now that we've stopped playing, stands
there with her girlfriend. I walk behind the stage, find a beer,
have a smoke, and Knut comes, finds a beer, has a smoke,
and then Knut says he'll go for a walk, look around for a bit,
we're going to stay over in the Youth Hall tonight, so he
should prepare a little for the night, he says, laughs, and
Knut takes a big swig of beer, and then I watch him walking
off. That girl, she has stood in front of the stage the whole
evening. I didn't dare to look at her, didn't want to catch her
eyes, and then, quite suddenly, and then we were there. I
drink beer, smoke. I stand up, say I want to stretch my legs a
little as well, I walk out on the stage, look out at the hall, and
I see Knut and the girl sitting on the bench along the wall
furthest away, and Knut's holding his arms around her
shoulders, and I see her leaning against Knut, but I can see
her body is stiff, and I go back, sit down behind the stage, get
another beer, and then the drummer says I shouldn't drink

so much, we haven't finished yet, have to wait for a bit, he
says, and I nod, just a little more, I say, sit down, drink beer,
and the drummer asks if something's wrong with me, my
eyes look so strange, he says, and I say no, it's nothing, and
then he says that we should start again soon, must find Knut,
must get going again now, he says, he knows what it's like
when Knut has fixed himself up, he forgets everything then,
he says, and then he goes off, comes back after a while, says
that I must come now, we'll get going with the playing again
now, and I stand up, walk out on the stage, pick up my guitar,
turn on the amplifier, and there she is, standing in front of
the stage, she and her girlfriend are standing there, and we're
playing again, the hall is full now, people are dancing, reeling
around, but she just stands there, in front of the stage.
Weekend after weekend, we carry the equipment out in the
old van, drive to some Youth Hall or other, carry it in, adjust
the sound, play, have a break, play, a beer and a smoke in the
break, and when we've finished, then there'd be a party,
weekend after weekend. That time, that girl. She stood in
front of the stage, the whole evening, she looked at me,
looked at Knut. Now I hear my mother coming up the stairs,
I sit here and write, and now my mother's coming, step by
step, what does she want now then, I hear her walking across
the floor. The restlessness is sinking in on me. She'll probably
tell me that I never go out anymore. Don't do anything. I
have to stop this writing, she'll say. I don't know. I don't go
out anymore. I haven't touched the guitar for a long time.
Don't know. My mother stands there in the doorway, she
knocked once, and then she opened the door, she looks at

me, asks what's this, why don't I ever come down anymore,
can't just sit here, have to go out, this won't do, before it was
the playing, at least, now, this. My mother stands in the
doorway. I look at her, look up, stop writing.

My mother just dropped in, she stroked my cheek, said I had
to stop this writing, had to go out, at least go to the shop,
could at least do a few playing jobs, she says, and then she
says she spoke to Knut's mother today, and she told her that
Knut's wife was dead. Knut's mother said that it was always
going to end badly. She couldn't see any other way, she said.
It was a while since she died. She was found, drowned. It
was terrible, Knut's mother said, but it had to end badly. It
was worst for the children, she said. It was probably suicide.
My mother stroked my cheek, asked me to come down. I
couldn't just sit here and write, she said. My mother just
dropped in. I had to come down, she said. I don't know. I
cannot bear this restlessness. My mother. I heard her steps
on the stairs. My mother is not all that old. Now this restlessness is unbearable. Accordingly I finish my writing.

Born in 1959 in Haugesund, in Vestland, western Norway, Jon Fosse's remarkably prolific career began in 1983 with his first novel, *Red, Black,* and since then he has published numerous novels, stories, books of poetry, children's books, and essay collections. He began writing plays in 1993, with *Someone Is Going to Come,* and since then he has written almost thirty plays, including *A Summer's Day, Dream of Autumn, Death Variations, Sleep,* and *I Am the Wind.* Since the mid-nineties his plays have had unparalleled international success, being performed over a thousand times all over the world; his works have been translated into more than fifty languages. Today Fosse is one of the most performed living playwrights, but he has continued to write novels, stories, and poetry of exceptional quality. In 2015, he received the Nordic Council Literature Prize for his work *Trilogy,* consisting of *Wakefulness, Olav's Dreams,* and *Weariness.* Fosse's earlier novels *Melancholy I and II, Morning and Evening,* and *Aliss at the Fire* have also received wide critical acclaim. Fosse received the 2023 Nobel Prize in Literature, and has been awarded numerous prizes both in Norway and abroad.

Dr. May-Brit Akerholt has extensive experience as a translator and production dramaturg of classic and contemporary plays. More than twenty of her translations have been produced by leading theatre companies around Australia and overseas. Her published translations include several plays by Ibsen and Strindberg; four volumes of plays by Jon Fosse (Oberon Books, London); three novels by Jon Fosse: *Boathouse, Trilogy*, and *An Angel Walks Through the Stage* (all by Dalkey Archive Press). She has written a book on Patrick White's drama and a number of her critical articles have been published in various books and journals.